The Treasure Trove of Stories and Poems

By: H. Yashnashree

Published By: FanatiXx Publication

The Treasure Trove of Stories and Poems

FanatiXx® Publication
AM/56, Basanti Colony, Rourkela 769012, Odisha

ISO 9001:2015 Certified

Copyright © H. Yashnashree

(2024)
All Rights Reserved.

The Treasure Trove of Stories and Poems

ISBN: 978-93-5605-315-1

Formatting & Design: My Authors Hub
MRP. 299/-
Typesetting By: BooksClub.in

No part of this publication may be reproduced, distributed, or transmitted in any form or by any means, including photocopying, recording, or other electronic or mechanical methods, without the prior written permission of the publisher, except in the case of brief quotations embodied in critical reviews and certain other non-commercial uses permitted by copyright law.

About Author

Ten-year-old Yashnashree studies at the **Bangalore International Academy (BIA) School.** She is a bibliophile and writer of stories; this is her second book. Her two passions are studying animal life and pursuing her dream of becoming a well-known author. Her favorite activities are badminton, Lego building, and swimming. She has won numerous writing contests hosted by Contestzeal and StoriesByChildren (portal).

In a national-level competition organized by IQ International Academy, she won first place in the essay writing category. In addition, IntellyJelly had given her a scholarship worth Rs. 6,000 in recognition of her write-up in a competition.

Dedication

To my mother, Saluja.M, who kindled the light of uniqueness through me.

To my father, Havish.V, who encouraged and supported me with literature.

To my two roosters, Sunshine and Meadow, who are extremely understanding of me.

To my grandparents Kasturi.V, Viswanath.B , Nalini.M and Murali.D, who gave me knowledge.

To my Uncle Dinesh.M and Aunt Saranya.D, who helped to generate numerous concepts for this book.

To my cousins Juanasree.D. and Lakshnashri.D, who listened to my stories with interest and enthusiasm.

To my Chairman sir, Dr. D. Muniraju and principal sir, Dr.P. Arokia Raj for your lifetime skills and indispensable knowledge to stand out.

H.Yashnashree

With particular gratitude to Storiesbychildren and to my mentor, Vardhini ma'am, who molded my talent to the surface.

I am grateful to my master, Lord Shirdi Sai Baba, for providing me with a wealth of creative ideas.

To every deity and teacher, for enablng me to overcome challenges.

Contents

About Author 3

Dedication 4

STORY

Story 1: THE FLIGHT OF FRIENDSHIP 11

Story 2: THE COURAGEOUS RABBIT 16

Story 3: THE TALE OF THE OPPOSITE EMOTIONS 19

Story 4: Unusual Friendship 23

Story 5: Meadow's diary (Non-Fiction story) 28

Story 6: Waking up in some country 32

Story 7: The waves 36

Story 8: THE story behind my name 44

Story 9: The twist of the poor to the rich 47

Story 10: The competition 50

Story 11: Adventure of sand castle 53

Story 12: Rose who turned into mother 56

Story 13: The real monster 62

Story 14: Why does the stars shine at night? 65

Story 15: A Lesson Which A Book Taught Me (Non-Fiction) ... 67

Story 16: The portion that was never told 69

Story 17: LEVEL UP PLANETS 76

    Introduction 76

    Chapter -1: The ...Alien 77

    Chapter 2 – The Comet's Tail 78

Chapter 3- A Ransom Kidnapping but Hidden 78

Chapter 4: The Hugest Mystery 79

Chapter 5:The Furious Duel 79

Chapter 6: Humbly, but the Truth "Stop right there." 80

Story 18: One day - One sec 83

Story 19: A Special Rescue Centre (essay) 87

Story 20: The courageous girl 90

Story 21: The mysterious adventure 93

Story 22: Catfish as meerkat (Dialogue writing) 98

Story 23: King Zeus Of Jupiter 106

Story 24: Grief- stricken time 109

Story 25: I have been stranded on a new planet 115

   Chapter 1: Meeting the Characters 115

   Chapter 2: Rainbow Outfits 117

   Chapter 3: Cultural Habitats in the Role 117

   Chapter 4: Twist 119

Story 26: The longest badminton shot 121

   Chapter 1: Introduction 121

   Chapter 2 :The Greatest Advice 123

   Chapter -3: Surprise party for the cheerleading 124

   Chapter–4: The racking session 125

   Chapter 5: The Fantastic Match Winner Is 126

Story 27: The Detective Agent 130

Story 28: Let the cat out of the bag 133

Story 29: Dear Diary 136

25-11-2023 136

27-11-2023 137

29-11-2023 138

1-12-2023 140

Story 30: THE AVENGE OF DEATH 142

Story 31: Friendship leads to mishaps at times 150

Story 32: Christmas story 159

Story 33: The Colosseum (ESSAY) 163

Story 34: The scarab of chambers 168

Story 35: The Revolutionary Change 177

    Chapter 1 : The Parchment Leads to misery 177

    Chapter 2: Desires with a Pail of Milk 179

    Chapter 3: Cookie on the Prowl 180

    Chapter 4: Glinting to where your heart desires 181

    Chapter 5: The debate of wishes 182

    Chapter 6: The change of name 184

    Chapter 7: Guidance from the fake 185

    Epilogue 188

Story 36: Monalisa 192

POEMS

Poem 1: The perfect summer break 203

Poem 2: I go to the city of Paris 207

Poem 3: AN AMUSEMENT DAY 209

Poem 4: My chicks 213

Poem 5: Friendship day	216
Poem 6: Independence Day and freedom	219
Poem 7: Teacher's Day	225
Poem 8: The Talking Blue Taipan	228
Poem 9: The natural garden and wonders of emphatize	230
Poem 10: Grandparents day	233
Poem 11: Inside shows	236
Poem 12: Shyness	239
Poem 13: A dirty fellow yellow shows his turn to shine	242
Poem 14: Widow's sorrow	245
Poem 15: Something no one knows…	247
Poem 16: Determination but feisty	249
Poem 17: Adventure in reading	251
Poem 18: Inner qualities pulverized or not	252
Poem 19: A drop can save a life	255
Poem 20: The pearly exchange	257
Poem 21: Diwali Celebration	261
Poem 22: The Whispers Of Tears	263
Poem 23: Time is valuable	265
Poem 24: Happy Thanks Giving	267
Poem 25: The wounds of courage	269
Poem 26: Obstacles	271
Poem 27 : Chase to be cherished	273
Poem 28: Who am I?	277

The Treasure Trove of Stories and Poems

Story 1:
THE FLIGHT OF FRIENDSHIP

Bamboo leaves are planted along the garden barks of trees. Honey dripped down its branches. Nearby the trees stood a majestic cottage bathed in the glow of the sun. The house had mushrooms everywhere, with a lane splattered with rain. The cottage looked a bit spooky. There was a huge hole that was not as far from the house. Inside, it was a fox that lived alone.

He was sly, funny, and smart. One evening, he decided to look into the cottage. He creaked open the door. Inside, he stood in awe. In front of him was a magical unicorn! Her pastel coloured mane and tail were more velvety and softer than his coat. The unicorn took no notice of him and vanished into thin air.

He was so curious to know where she had gone. He walked in, threading the floor silently. He noticed a huge bookshelf and raced over it. Near it was an armchair, and sitting on it was the unicorn. She had reading glasses placed on her eyes and was very focused as she opened the book. The fox looked at her with pleading eyes and slowly whispered," Could I read this book with you?" The unicorn was first surprised at being spied. But then she waved her hand and beckoned for him to sit with her. The fox curled up with the unicorn and they started from page one. They opened the page and saw a huge hole that was ready to suck them in." Ready", the unicorn voiced out. "Yes," verbalized the fox determinedly.

The unicorn and the fox placed their paws and hoofs together, "Ready to start a new adventure". It soon became black, and when they opened their eyes, they found themselves floating on a huge cloud. When rainbows sprouted over her, the duo tried to touch it. The unicorn successfully sat on it, sliding up and down. She excitedly signaled for the fox to follow her. The fox tried to do the same, but he got melted by the rainbow. She was afraid for her friends, so she turned back and touched the rainbow. But, sadly, she didn't disappear. Instantly, the book slammed shut, and they came back to their normal lives. The fox said, "I think this book is humdrum". The unicorn felt sad and was about to say something, when he interrupted her. "I will go choose another book", the fox put into the words. He found a huge, thick tome called 'THE FLIGHT OF FRIENDSHIP'. He placed the book on the table and looked for another. He found a book called' Do Your Own Story'. He glanced at the unicorn and asked, "Which book should I read?". The unicorn looked at both of it and replied, "It's the big tome". The fox unconvincingly gawped at the tomb and stated, "What is the book of doing your own story?". That is personal which I cannot show you", the unicorn expressed.

The fox became heartbroken and kept the book aside. She glimpsed at the tomb with a defeated sigh and told, "May I come tomorrow to read it?" The unicorn held his hand and spoke, "Yes, but you should read this story of what you have selected and that is the rules of my house". The fox took one glare at his gentle friend and nodded his head.

The next morning, they took the tomb book, and when they opened it inside, it was ready to suck them in. Again, it became black, and when he went into the story, he was in an enchanted forest. There was a spare of mushrooms, which always recommended him not to go near them. When he looked at his paws, he saw that the aging process was reversed. He soon became a kit. A kind aging old lady took care of him in a cottage near the woods.

The kit one night ran outside to play by himself, but he saw a pair of glamorous mushrooms gleaming outside. He went to lick it, but the old lady said, "No". He ran angrily towards the mushrooms and licked them. He vanished...

The old lady stood in a fixed posture and started crying. She did not know that her fox cub was completely safe. In the meantime, inside the mushroom was a fairy department that had lost their way from the cloud kingdom. They were trying all they could to reach the cloud kingdom.

The kit went inside the mushroom and saw the unicorn. He went closer and sniffed a fairy. The fairy was terrified. The kit found tubes and pipes connecting to every single room, and fairies were in every single tube. The kit barked and began to race with a fairy. He was about to run and caught up with a fairy as it went into a tube. It was a little slippery and slidy, but it didn't demolish the courage to catch the fairy. When he reached the end of the room, he saw a beautiful unicorn playing with the fairies. He immediately raced up to it, but he did not see what was going to happen. The unicorn did not know what to do and opened a huge portal, where the kit ran and was stuck inside. The unicorn felt a great sympathy rising in her and dove off inside her own portal. Soon, inside her own portal, the unicorn saved the kit from a dangerous and spooky ghost. Before the ghost came to claw them, they escaped inside the unicorn's portal. So, they arrived in front of all the fairies.

The unicorn came closer to the kit and pushed his nose away. When their noses touched, they felt reunited. They both began flying, were surrounded by love and unity, and helped themselves to get over it. All the fairies sat on the kit, and the unicorn thankfully flew away into the sky. Soon, the fairies reached the cloud kingdom and enjoyed their stay. Later, they dropped the kit in the enchanted forest, where they all lived in harmony and peace.

THE END

H.Yashnashree

Story 2:
THE COURAGEOUS RABBIT

Ahh! a shriek came as some rocks came rolling down a hill. The rocks had come from a burrow. Out popped a rabbit from the burrow who was chuckling to himself. Since yesterday a pesky boy with freckles had put his hand inside the burrow five times a day. Getting annoyed Puggle the rabbit bit the boy and asked," Why do you keep poking your hand inside my burrow?". The boy replied," I kept my grandpa's gold bricks here because I was angry at him, but now it is not there. Puggle consoled him and told, "It is fine with me if I could help you get your gold back. The boy said, "It would be a pleasure if I could give you something in return". "I know what! you could give me some carrots as a gift", replied the rabbit. He bounced off into the woods echoing, "I will be back". Puggle took a swift turn and headed right. Suddenly he felt a stab of poke on his hips. Swiftly said, "You are now my prey". Swiftly flew the rabbit to the flower garden where his den was. Swiftly put the rabbit in a large prison with one window but without any bars.

In the corner was a pile of gold bricks. The happy rabbit said, "Who hoo! Jackpot!". Puggle decided to rest for a while. In the meantime, the rabbit heard the cackling of the evil vulture who was replied to several vulture's wing beats and heard that they were planning to eat him for dinner. Without thinking the rabbit did a backflip and flew out of the window. He saw a hole and peeked. A familiar snout popped out. It was Hamlet the mouse, the rabbit's old friend. Puggle told Hamlet all about his adventures and asked him a favor, "Could Hamlet and his family crawl inside the window and get the blocks of gold inside?". Hamlet replied, "Of course! We would love to!" Hamlet and his family marched up the wall and slowly one by one came down holding the gold bricks on their back. The official head of Hamlet's family measured the rabbit and weaved him a coat, hat and backpack, saying," Bye, Puggle left for his burrow. He happily gave the gold bricks back to the boy who gave him dozens of carrots and thanked him profusely and left. Puggle winked to himself and helped himself with the carrots.

The Treasure Trove of Stories and Poems

Story 3:
THE TALE OF THE OPPOSITE EMOTIONS

The fog descended with grey clouds, making the atmosphere very eerie. The waves as it tried to jump out of reach. The air was moist and was about to pour rain. The fog became so terrible that nobody could see themselves. There was an outline of a ship that glided on the water. The cruise was sandy with the scratches of the name 'Dancing Waves'. As the cruise dangerously wobbled in the Atlantic Ocean, the waves seemed to be more enthusiastic. The captain, Andrew, tried to keep the waves at bay while his confident Liam, who was a sailor and his best mate, tried to contact other ships. Captain Andrew was short-tempered, mean-spirited, and very smart in languages and vocabulary, while Liam was energetic and kind. Liam looked out of the foggy window and saw something falling towards them and he heard a scream.

Liam pocketed his handkerchief and cantered towards a circular room. The room was enormous, with marble pillars holding the aesthetic tapestries of war and battle. It was the great hall of the ship. On the far end of the ball, there stood a gigantic glass painting of the captain and his crew. There was a scrum of people admiring a few paintings and porcelain objects that were placed around the room. There was another huge scrum where a Victorian lady had fallen unconscious. Liam gingerly pushed through the crowd and demanded to know what had happened.

But when he said that sentence, everybody scrambled away from the Victorian lady. Liam looked through a porthole in another direction and to his great astonishment, found a hurricane blowing out over the horizon. He quickly left the area and told the captain what had happened. The captain was bomb shelled to hear the news and became scared about his safety. What could he do? In raging anger, he slammed the keyboard of his computer, muttering curses. He was a very bad captain, but Liam, who was kind-hearted, never mentioned that to the captain. He told himself that the captain ought to learn a lesson himself. He commanded Liam and said, "How can I make sure that none of the passengers know about this hurricane?". Liam became thoughtful at this point. He had no good ideas and he thought he might anger the captain even more. He thought to himself, "What probably was the easiest method of manipulating the passengers?". He told the captain that he was very thirsty and would hitch up a drink on his way to the porthole so that he could see the distance of the hurricane.

Meanwhile, he hoped that he would get a good idea. Suddenly, he noticed a bed sliding off the cabin. It was coming straight to Liam. Liam felt dizzy about the problems and felt senseless. Instantly, the boat was hit with a dusty gale. The captain no longer cared for the ship but only for his life and he left control of the ship. He ran to the lifeboat area and hoped for one of them. When his staff landed him, he secretly rowed away into the night. All of a sudden, he heard a crash in his boat, and his leg got stuck due to a rock, but no one could see him in this fog. He began to scream for help. Liam soon came to his senses and made everybody sit in the lifeboat, and tried to steer them away. When he realized they were safer on the ship, he made them get back to the ship, as the hurricane was pretty far away. He heard the captain's voice from a distance and went after him. Liam rescued the captain using an anchor, and the captain apologized for being jealous, and then they escaped the hurricane. Soon they rowed into the starry night and defeated the hurricane from reaching the ship. When the survivors reached home, the captain apologized for not helping the people first. Liam soon wrote the story about the survivors reaching land safely and it became a wonderful story of friendship.

The Treasure Trove of Stories and Poems

Story 4:
Unusual Friendship

Bam! Crash! Wham!

I skidded off the diving board. I fainted as my coach caught me. The next thing he did was throw a bucket of salty, mucky water.

This was my first swimming class, OOPS! I noticed everybody clicking at me. Ohh! Why do I get humiliated on the first day?

The coach told me to swim rather than dive.

I agreed.

But I dived.

Then I swam as fast as I could.

I heard something detecting me.

I inhaled faster.

I saw something kaleidoscopic. I was about to have a go at it, so I could observe it.

I knew something was near me. I immediately started having a countdown for something.

1...2...3...4...

Something promptly gobbled me up! The illumination went black.

5…6…7…8…

Suddenly, a jaw sprang out. I remembered that I had gone to gymnastics before.

9…

I was near the whale's face. It opened its wide mouth. I dogged all of the sharp, pointy teeth, and it pushed me inside carefully with its slobbery tongue.

10… Thud!
I thudded on the belly and had rolled my way to the tail, trying to figure a way out. It was a calamitous place.

Suddenly, the whale swallowed a gallon of water. I was horror-struck. I instantly counted backward.

10…9…8…7…

I saw something. A blowhole!

Straight away, a light bulb came to mind. Ting!

6…5…4…3…

I went where the hole was and got sucked in. But to my horror, I was stuck. My idea went down the drain.

2…Thump!

I fell down. I had to get out, but how? I crawled back to the belly, staring dreamily at the blowhole, trying to make a plan.

...1...(z...z...z..)

Third, I felt that I could understand the whale. I felt he muttered to me that he was alone. I soothed him with my gentle voice, uttering, "It's okay". I finally voiced out, How did I get into its belly, and if it could let me go?" As if understanding, it took a swift upward step and opened its jaws!

Pump! Pump! Pump!

My heart pumped faster. I swam jitterily. I popped out. The whale I had been with turned to me and let me touch his body. We two touched! The killer shark and me! It heaved me on its back, and I lounged as we came to the surface. The coach gasped, a few children fainted, and one child even pressed the alarm.

Instantly, the police came. The coach fell to his knees and bellowed, Sorry! Please". "Why is he saying that? The children began to whisper. A police officer came up to them and began to explain," Your coach is a fraud, and there is an ocean below. He built this swimming pool on top of it, so whenever he doesn't like any child, he will open the cages of whales so one will eat the child. After that, he lies to the respective parents that he saved the child on a swim trip but has suffered death!".

There was an awkward silence! I was sad that my friend was gone. During summer break, I and my parents went to Hawaii. At the beach, a wave splashed all over me. I looked up to a

Fountain -- No

Rock -- No

Whale -- YES

It was a whale that let me touch his body. I realized, Humpty!" (his new name). I learned how to surfboard, and then I collected seashells out of it. I used a blue string to sew it together as a BHAFF (Best Human Animal Friend Forever). I always carry a needle and coloured strings for emergencies. "I Miss You", I hugged the whale, and in return, he grunted.

While we were back home, Mom gave me the best surprise, a whale tooth Minecraft machine.

H.Yashnashree

Story 5:
Meadow's diary (Non-Fiction story)

Today was 26/11/23 Sunday. My instinct told me that today was my monthly bath. I wondered how my younger brother Sunshine was able to handle the cool prickly water. Our mother had put him on his back. On this crispy morning, I, Meadow the rooster decided nothing should happen wrong today. I decided to annoy my parents, my younger brother Sunshine, the rooster and my older sister Yashna. After my mother released us from the basement room, my brother and I began to run and quarrel. At 1 o clock my mother had received a call from us when we were not eating so our mother fed us affectionally. Our mom was always fed up with me because I never ate anything and played always. Sunshine always eats everything. My mother shouted at me, "Come on Meadow, this has been the 10th time before you have eaten anything". I knew my sister Yashna was just like me but not always like that. After I ate just 6 spoons of my curry, my sister emerged from the house. It was actually mid-afternoon. Sunshine and I had gone to different nook of the garden but I had laid down for a snooze when my mother and my sister decided to take up photos of me. I wanted to say "Couldn't you have taken a photo of Sunshine?". My mother rushed inside the home to grab the phone. Meanwhile the maid and our mother were screaming at each other and my sister was making more uneasy and begging to sit where I was, but after hearing the loud screams and commotions I rose up uneasily then I started walking with Sunshine chatting with him. Then my sister told to our mother you should have come earlier because Meadow got up. After 10 minutes my sister had something in her hand when she emerged out. My mother was disappointed and went into the house for a while. Just after 2 minutes again my sister came out holding something curious in her hand. "I guess I can enroll you in a competition if you are willing to participate "Our sister told us. After teaching us a few magic tricks and we ate the rest of the onions pieces from her hand. I was so happy with the snack and so was my brother Sunshine too. After everyone's lunch, my mother and my sister emerged out together. My sister was holding a hairdryer and a bucket in each hand.

My mother was holding a strawberry scented shampoo which Sunshine had used for his bath. I thought even more worse had come. I thought my parents had forgotten about my bath today. But they hadn't. My mother cuddled me like an infant. I started to whimper then something cool touched my body. My mother drenched me in cool water. My sister mixed the shampoo with water. So I knew my bath time was ready. I wriggled, scuttled and ran away from my parents. Again my father chased me around and pounced on me again. I was caught very harshly and given to my mother then I was cuddled like an infant. Our father held me harshly and made me to sit like a duck in the middle of the pavement. As I was drenched in shampoo water, my sister took some pictures of me and wrote a word say," Meadow has a bath". She showed it to my parents. After my sister wiped me in a rough towel, my father held me as usual like a duck in the basement on the stone stool. My mom turned on the hair dryer and made me warm. Finally exhausted and warmed from the warmth of the air dryer. I myself sat like a duck. Obediently, my sister again started taking photos of me. I started liking the warmth of the air dryer. Our mother told to my sister to go and get some walnuts which is my favorite. But my father had avoided taking the walnuts. So my sister stole some walnuts and came running into the basement. She pieced the walnuts and divided to me and Sunshine. But I got the more treats. After my sister broke the walnuts equally I loved the taste with interest and happiness. After munching the walnuts, my mother cuddled me like an infant again.

My mother took me out and made me sleep under her grateful arms. She was so affectionate when she strokes me. My mom whispered," Meadow and sunshine, you two are the best roosters in this world. I love you". Again my sister took a photo of me. After which looked like 25 minutes I broke my sleep in a start and jumped away. My sister consoled Sunshine that she will take photos of him when he takes a bath. Our sister wasn't allowed to see sunshine's bath so she couldn't do anything grand like me. My sister vowed Sunshine that she could do everything what she did for me. So this is the end of my favorite bath.

H.Yashnashree

Story 6:
Waking up in some country

Slam! The angel of the humanity shut the window. She flew off to her bookshelf and chose her tome. She went through it for an empty page and dipped her quill in her aqua colour ink. She wrote a huge description of someone.

I was about to fall asleep when a pair of eyes peeped in the window. I felt my blood run cold. I felt like being thrown on rubble. I woke up in the morning with bruises. All the houses I saw had slanting roofs which was really odd.

I realized something was wrong. As I had never been to this place. I sat down on the ground and that was when a light bulb clicked.

I walked down a street and found a rag in a corner. I took it and wore it on top. I marched towards the famous and historical building named Peace Wing and White Wing.

I timidly walked in and the counter assistant looked shocked and immediately escorted me to the dormitory. I was about to break down into bits and cry until dawn, when the door flung open, I wondered then as I could see new roommates.

Peace wing and White Wing is a concrete building where they adopt orphans and street kids to heal and get adopted to the right family. There came a chubby-looking girl, wearing a different type of hairstyle. She was wearing a fox pattern skirt with an orange T-shirt. Her name was Ahana. Next, came a girl with brown hair which was curly and she wore glasses. Her name was Parker. As we awkwardly shuffled back to our beds, in a thrice, Ahana sharply whispered in my ear," Are you an Indian?". I gave her a frightened look and quietly nodded. Ahana sweetly replied back, "Even I am an Indian". I bizarrely cocked my head at her and voiced, "What are you doing here?". Ahana shushed and said, "I will tell you later". I curiously looked at her and then glided away to the library. Over there, I took an interesting book from the shelf and was about to flip the first page, when two pieces of paper slipped out, one was written, "Bun Bun Cargo" and the other was penned, "Cafa Café restaurant and tea".

I slipped the paper into my pocket and took it back to the dormitory. Parker looked at me and Ahana curtly and sighed. Ahana looked at me razzing and mocked," You haven't got the paper. Have you?". Ahana looked at me sarcastically and said," Never mind that's nothing". I rolled my eyes and told her everything. She hesitated for a moment and replied, "I am Indian as well as Tamilian and I was kidnapped at night. I had always had a dream of escaping and seeing the world. I sadly had never ever thought of that until now. It feels bad to have been dumped in the middle of the world".

"Same, but I am a Bengalurian. I was as well kidnapped", I aired.

Parker curiously sat between us and declared, "I am from USA. I had been kidnapped when I had gone to bed". "Really!!!", Ahana exclaimed. Ahana crumpled a paper from her pocket to take it out. Aahana dipped her pen and knocked it out.

"Does anyone want to create an escape plan? Does anyone have creative writing skills? They are known as writers", Ahana determined.

I held up my hand and said, "I am a writer". I racked my brain and announced," I have an idea". I immediately snatched the pen and shifted the paper and started drawing a plan. Once I completed it, Parker and Ahana had said that it was a marvelous plan.

Parker always wanted to become an actress so she had her own cloak in the cupboard. It fitted perfectly. So they were ready to put their plan into action.

Parker rushed with her cloak and begged the caretaker named Fickle to take her to the museum. Everybody might not want us to go. But after begging, thankfully, Parker was allowed to go. She smuggled both of them into the cloak and successfully found out the two places where helping the charity and hostel of the Peace wing and White wing.

Delightfully, I picky-pocked their tickets, then, me, Parker and Ahana went back home.

H.Yashnashree

Story 7:
The waves

The waves up roared and splashed at his feet. The sand merrily wiped at his feet. The gale blew high, sending a rush of happiness onto the boy's head, sending his blonde, trusty hair fly strands of hair backward. The sand, which was greyish, mixed with the water and formed salty waves that fell on the boy's blue checked shirt. His rosy-like timber lips showed the agony of being alone. He could not go into the seaside house that was presented in chalky white with wet bricks and patches of paint falling. He made up his mind that he was not going in. The people who owned this place had hidden him from the world. Nobody knew that they were laboring kids like him in that place. He knew it was wrong to be labored. As a kid, he was taken into consideration as a servant. He had a pang of jealousy for the adults, who had their own petty lives while they worked for them. He immediately knew his name. He remembered that he had a nickname, Aarick. It meant being a lone ruler or a lone Viking. He was even as strong as a Viking, let alone his name.

Soon, his nickname became his actual name. He was as tired as a dark cloud, unable to hold his tears, which were rain. After one last gale, there came the rain splattering down his face. Feeling drowsy, Aarick squeezed his wadded -up shirt full of water and tramped into the back door. He had to find his way into the servant's cabin. He didn't want to bump into his master or mistress, for they whipped him with a fan or hard cane. He was unlike a horse wanting to be whipped to make him move. He was thankful that their master had not bought a flexible whip that was sharp enough to make anyone bleed.

He had a few friends who were kind to him from the start. He was not so sure how he could get in without their master or mistress seeing him. He had the caliber to cheat them. Hoodwinking them made him happier at thought. In the backyard, there was his friend, Perrywinkle. She was 13 years old. She was an expert in gardening and was a gardener for their courtyards. Perrywinkle's brown hair was drenched in the rain, and he was merrily smiling, putting seeds in the soil. Aarick was 10 years old and was himself the butler for his master and mistress.

Being a butler, he was not treated as harshly as the others'. He was the main servant out of everyone. Perrywinkle gazed at Aarick and whispered, "Hey Butler Aarick, I see something is coming into your mind." Aarick gave a mischievous twinkle in his eyes. Aarick whistled back, "Tell me when you have finished sowing." Perrywinkle gleamed at him, "I have already wrapped up my work. Let's go according to your beat". Perrywinkle had a trolley of seeds and beckoned Aarick to jump inside it. Aarick smiled at her and jumped inside, covered in chucks of seeds. He had not been seen. When she pushed the trolley and came to a halt in front of the servant's cabin, he emerged and pushed himself inside the door. There was a huge gossip in the servant's cabin, and everyone was excited to tell Aarick, something interesting. The carriage master was a young boy who was 9 years old named Christoper. He said that the master and mistress were pleased with your work. Tomorrow they are cutting a cake for your birthday and having a surprise field trip for you. We are all accompanying you as well.

Aarick knew no bounds of happiness erupting within him. He was excited for the day ahead of him. He wondered what kind of cake it was going to be. He saw everyone having a twinge of jealousy towards him for being main and loved because he always did his work correctly without arguing with anyone. This made him special to the master and mistress.

Aarick immediately washed his face, cleansed his arms, and wore his torn blue checked shirt with his purple pants. At once, he cuddled himself to his bed and was fast asleep on the rags before he knew it. The next day, his master and mistress were excited for Aarick and had given him a bunch of new clothes. The clothes were very expensive, but they were from a thrift store.

Aarick liked himself so much in the mirror that he wished to wear clothes like that every day. After blowing out his candles on the birthday cake, which was Belgian chocolate, he cut them into large pieces and gave them to the mistress and master. After giving it to them, he fed himself and his friends with the cake. Everyone loved the taste of it, and they all packed the picnic bag to go to the forest.

All the kids were whipped by the mistress and master for packing the food. When the food was packed, the master and mistress cruelly pushed everyone and hit a few to start moving the carriage in which Aarick and their owner were sitting in the front seat. Aarick couldn't help but said to himself that he was a little cruel, and Aarick noticed that he, his mistress, and his master looked the same.

When they reached the forest camp, all of them were very excited and started to unpack without heeding any advice. The master and mistress took him for a walk, and on their way there, they confessed that Aarick was actually their son, and they knew that everyone would blame him. They did not want him to suffer because of them. They abandoned him because they wanted a girl child and used him as a slave, but now the master and mistress were asking for mercy.

Aarick yelled at them," What I heard now must be fake. I don't want to think of you as my parents. You are the cruelest parents in the world. I have done nothing to deserve slavery from you". He stormed off to join his friends to go to the circus.

Meanwhile....

God had set foot on the regretful and guilty birthday of Aarick. God disguised himself as a girl in his twenties and had dropped a gift of unexpected joy. God knew the one thing that would make him happy, and he solemnly walked off.

Aarick pounced on the circus tent. He first saw on the grass that laid a wrapped box. His curiosity knew no bounds and wanted to remove and see what was inside. He immediately tore open it, and there lay a gem of happiness. When he wore it, he did not know it was God's lesson for him.

In a thrice, the box sucked him into the world of happiness, where no labor was committed. The land was full of people smiling, and he became ecstatic and got around with everyone. He was friendly, and soon he smothered a smile. After a few hours, he wanted his normal life, as he realized that God can give happiness and sadness to those he loves. But when he was joyful, he started running to a porthole, which he found, and decided to go through it to go home. When he went, his leg slipped and his hands were grabbed, and half of it became stony and the rest was active and bouncy. Soon he slipped and fell unconscious, unable to retrieve himself again.

Aarick felt himself leaving the world and begged God to catch him on his way. God did exactly what he wanted. Meanwhile, Aarick's wicked parents were unable to wash their sins away and were angrily searching the whole place.

The kids, meanwhile, evacuated from the circus to help with the search. Nobody was too interested in the master and mistress' wishes. But, of course, they were worried about their butler friend. Everyone cried their hearts out, but for some reason, their mistress and master thought it was Christoper who had not been taken care of Aarick. They whipped him so hard on Christoper's neck that he left the world. Up aboard in heaven, there came Aarick, who was looking miserable and murmured to himself, "I just want to go back to my parents. I don't find God so good in heaven.

Aarick was accidentally transported to heaven as he was caught by God. Aarick would not help, but he was in a rage with God. He could not feel his heart burn at the sight of God, but he was miserably longing to go back to his parents, whom only he saw in his bad eyes and never felt so great in his good eyes. This time, he had met them with good eyes and wanted to be back with his parents. But his heart burned at the thought of being slaved by his parents.

He could not believe the facts about his parents, nor neither him. He saved himself up to a hill where God was inviting new invitees to join in at heaven. In the queue, Aarick spotted someone facially familiar and went up to see him. But then he realized it was Christoper. "What is Christoper doing in heaven? Could he be searching for me?", Aarick thought.

Christoper smiled and fell to God's knees. He looked up to see Aarick in front of God. "Aarick, you made me die because you hid over here, and you have got me killed by the master and mistress",Christoper yelled in despair. Aarick had a cruel motivation inside his heart and dare not let it out, and the moment Aarick got angry at Christoper, he snapped his teeth and growled angrily. Aarick begged God to leave him home, but God sighed and left him home in despair.

God had lost Aarick just for the sake of happiness but decided to watch his next move. As soon as God lowered Aarick into the forest, he watched Aarick's next move. Aarick noticed the circus was over and the carriage where it had been parked had been taken away, and he was confused.

As soon as Aarick did not know what to do, God squeezed through the clouds and held him gently and smiled," I knew you could not go further than you have. You can be here with me, but first wash away your own sins before committing a crime against them. I know you very well and no longer that your parents need you at home. As far as I know, they will be punished in a short time. You may now go and meet Christoper, whom you have been talking to as a friend. Now ask me a boon I may grant you unless it is not about your parents".

"God, I have mistaken that you cannot read my mind. But, of course, you have been knowing that in my mind I wish I was as cruel as my parents. I promise you this sin will not be committed. Please, will you wash away my sins and teach me the Bible scroll? All the rhythms must be in my heart except for the cruelness, which should be squeezed away", Aarick responded.

"My dear child, your sins are reversible, as you have regretted them, how about your parents?" God voiced out.

Aarick and God gazed at each other gravely, but they knew that his parents' next life was not as great and cruel as their past life. "They will soon learn their lesson, as their incredible son has", God pointed out to Aarick.

Somehow, his parents could not find him anywhere and were convinced that he had been killed by some wild animals. To sort it out, they tried to find him. They regretted the part where their son was a slave for them. They could not last their long life and knew that they were going to die, and of course they died very soon in the hope of having their son again.

H.Yashnashree

Story 8:
THE story behind my name

Friday 16 August 2013, a woman staggered into a hospital with her man and her parents with her long, flowing black crop of hair waving side to side. She went in with her man and parents to a chalky yellow hospital by the name of BALAJI NURSING. The glass door was open so the bright sun's rays would flood in. It was 11:00 am when the group of people had come in. As they stepped in, they noticed an attractive Chinese floral design welcome mat neatly placed on the floor. They walked on the pearly white tiles, which gave a squeaky noise when each step was placed.

A nurse approached them and the lady was ushered inside the room where she gave birth to a baby girl at 6:16 pm. The baby girl was me YASHNA! The woman's parents were my grandparents! This is how I was born.

Every child's first question will be," Mother, what is the story behind my name?". Not every child clarifies their name, but I have gotten clarification. So …. Listen on!

May 18, 2014, was my naming ceremony. In the morning, it was shining brightly. I was 9 months old. I woke up at 8:00 am and started waiting because of not have much sleep.

H.Yashnashree

My mother consoled me, brushed my teeth, bathed me, and decked me up with jewels and a green pink-dress. My mom carried me downstairs and the rituals of my naming ceremony started. In the end, everyone whispered Yashnashree in my ear as a custom.

In my family, there are lots of customs, mostly in names. So now I will share them....

Everybody in my family has 5 names. My five names are H. Yashnashree, Yashita, Tejonidha, Skandashri, and Lakshanya. My mom searched in many mythological books to find names starting with 'Y' because my grandma, the astrologer said that I was born on the Leo star, so it must be Y.

My mom wanted my name to be unique and with fewer syllables. She got some of my names from Google too. I wish I had 30 names so people could call each of them each day of the month! I was born at the Varamahalakshmi festival, so my last name is Shree. My mother was the happiest person when I got my name. This is how I got my name.

The Treasure Trove of Stories and Poems

46

H.Yashnashree

Story 9:
The twist of the poor to the rich

Reels fell from the camera as a man picked them up. He then headed to the tent with it. His hands were bony and sharp. Photography was brimmed in his heart, he knew he was multitalented but he could not think of a day left out without his camera. As he booked tickets and went to places taking his tent and guinea pig and there were many professional photographers who always got the money and he was unable to find anybody interested in his photography. His passion almost ruined him. Soon later he felt like giving up but he thought about another job which should help him succeed in everything. He soon was running of out money and therefore, the ticket to happiness and amount of love was cherished by his pet, a guinea pig, to cheer him up. The man was named Robert, and the guinea pig was named Corn Puff. Robert closed his eyes and remembered the timeline of his life. When he was three, he used to ring the bell at the church. When he was seven, he was trained to sell peach juice, and when he was thirteen, he used to make candles or paintings.

He was alright with his money, but he knew that he also had to pay the debts for renting his tent. It was hard to say that he was indigent, but he had to admit what life was like. He started to come up with a great idea that would help him not become penniless. Out of the blue, he had a mind-blowing idea that surely helped him get through his trouble. He first decided to start begging for paper; once he started, it felt like a dream because his idea was amazing. He began to beg for alms and soon noticed that since there was no payment at all, people commenced and gave him the papers he needed.

Once he was completed, with the help of his guinea pig, they initiated to get one card for five strokes of the guinea pig. Once Robert got the lucky customer, his guinea pig had a good massage as he examined the greeting card. At once, he had twenty seven cards and wrote on each of them his plans and carnivals that he was going to prepare. He begged an architect for money for his carnival. The kind-hearted person had given him the money he needed. Once he opened his own carnival games, people started flocking in to buy paintings, mostly on the themes of winter and candles. They also bought peach juice and their photos from Robert. They also heard marvelous tales of ancient relics like globes and bells.

He soon became richer and smarter, filled with love and devotion for his job and Corn Puff. He rewarded the architect by giving him a wondrous idea of the architecture of the building. From now on, he has learned a valuable lesson that not to give up until you achieve something.

H.Yashnashree

Story 10:
The competition

The three girls were very excited to compete with the three boys. The older one was called Lisa. The middle one was called Mia. The youngest one was Molly. They are sisters. The boys who they had to compete for are, the older one called John. The second one was called Paul. The youngest one was Jack. John and Lisa had to drive a super motor car. Lisa and her sisters decided on a plan. When the referee Mr Grankger blew the whistle, the supercar drove ahead. Lisa had built a superfast car machine. She had on it and zoomed faster than others. John wondered how could she ride so fast. He knew something was fishy with Lisa. Then he screamed," Lisa, the finishing line is over there." When Lisa turned the way, John was heading, John saw the superfast machine. Then John chuckled to himself. That way is for the forest. Then he drove straight and won the competition. Next was, Mia and Paul's turn. They had to fly an aeroplane. They had given a special aeroplane suit. Mia chose yellow pant with two small pockets, an olive-green warm jacket, pink boots and flying glasses which straps to the ears. Paul chose violet pants, a violet shirt with an aeroplane badge, yellow headphones, clear glasses and yellow boots. They sat in the aeroplane seats and flew. Paul wanted to impress the judge. He did loop the loop and he fell from the aeroplane. Hia caught him. They flew to the judges while the plane crashed. Mia won the competition. Jack got his skating boots and Molly got hers too. They started to skate in the skating rink. They had to impress the judges. Molly did her ballerina steps which she learnt at skating. Jack did some funky dance moves that were amazing. That time while he was trying a cartwheel, he suddenly fell to the ground and broke his legs. Finally, Molly won. When the two sisters came after the competition. They asked," Where is Lisa" to John. John chuckled to himself. Poor Lisa she went into the forest. Oh no we have to save Lisa. Molly and Mia jumped into an extra car and drew to the forest route. There they found Lisa. "What happened Lisa, why are you crying?", Lisa said," John tricked me by saying the forest route is the finishing line". "Oh my god! John is the tricker", Mia said. They took her back. Lisa told the truth that she also had been using the super fast machine. Molly said the whole truth to the judges. The judges said," I have a special announcement to make. No one wins the car competition . The reward that John received will be taken away". The girls were happy that they had won everything except Lisa. They went home to eat chocolates and ice cream. The boys went home sobbing.

H.Yashnashree

Story 11:
Adventure of sand castle

Grace sat back and regarded her sand castle proudly. She lay down on her towel, thinking how nice it would be to live in a castle. She closed her eyes. When she opened them again, the castle towered above her and the door was open. Grace stared at the huge brass door's shiny knob where there was a signboard saying that visitors were allowed. Grace felt a zap of excitement and curiosity surge through her. She walked on the silky red mat with golden laces which was heading to the mouth of the castle. At the entrance of the castle, ferocious guards were standing with funny feather tufts on their helmets. They stared at Grace coldly and smirked. One guard put his spear down and asked," Who are you"?. Grace replied," I am a visitor and want to explore the castle". The guards put their spears down and warned in a steely voice," Be careful". Grace skipped and strolled through the entrance of the castle to bump into a golden, elegant, charming statue that was a grateful lady. "Wow", said Grace in awe. The slamming of doors interrupted her. She stared at a copper door which was written in sunny yellow, 'UNIVERSE GALAXY'. Grace got curious and ran inside. Inside was a swing attached to a telescope around that was the whole universe!!!. The bright stars, the planets, the silver moon, the golden sun, the dusty nebulas, the fiery comets, the stony meteors, and the colorful galaxies swirled around it. She sat on the swing and swung with her mouth open. Soon, she felt the surprisement go out of her body and walked out of the door. Before she could see, she fainted. When she opened her eyes, they tied her to the wall near a cackling black pot of fluidity, sloppy shrimp pink soup. Suddenly, a pale-faced witch and wizard appeared from nowhere. The witch said," Now I can kill that girl!!!". The wizard yelled," Wait, she should have her glory day before she dies". Without thinking, Grace asked for a swing. Grace swung violently, which knocked out the witch who had to cross her. The wizard rushed to the witch and pulled out his wand. Grace took the wand out of the wizard's hand and said, "Kill them. In a moment the witch and wizard were dead". In a second, a sage appeared and said, "There are two wishes to let you go". Grace replied," Okay!, first, how did you come, and whose place is this?. The sage chuckled and said," I am Ageo and your determination of killing witch and wizard has freed the prisoners by heart. This is my castle. I am a hidden prince ".Grace replied," Cool!, second, let me go home". Ageo took a magical bottle and splashed it on her. Her eyes became blurry. When she opened her eyes, her brother Tom yelled," Are you okay"?. "Yeah", replied Grace in a slow coughing voice. Her brother and parents scooped her up into a tight hug and explained," A blue nave wave crept behind you and hurtled all over and you fainted."Grace interrupted and told them her story." Cool", her family told and happily went home.

H.Yashnashree

Story 12:
Rose who turned into mother

A rich marathon couple had three daughters: Orchid, Lily, and Rose. Rose, the youngest at school and home, was annoyed and ignored by her other sisters. Orchid wore a big bun on her head. Rose wore two ponytails and black square glasses. Lily had free curly black hair. Rose was the smartest one in the class. Orchid was the popular girl at school and Lily was good at sports. The three sisters were liked for their characters. The school was one of the most famous in the world. When Lily, Orchid, and Rose were grownups (Rose was 20, Lily was 26 and Orchid was 34). During that time, their father had gone for a job in Washington. He would come after 5 years, that time Orchid and Lily came up with a Evilest plan. They decided to put Rose in Exile for 5 years. Rose sadly understood the plan but she knew that she would certainly allow to stay there whenever she wanted. Rose was very intelligent to understand the actions of her sisters but she listens to them. So, she left the next morning without telling anyone. But left a small note in which it said," I will come back surely one day. I am leaving now." Rose packed a lot of food so that she would not feel hungry and also took some money along with her. Everyone on the road loved Rose. Everyone knew about the exile as Lily and Orchid had announced it. They were all sad and droopy as Rose hummed to the destination. She went deeper and deeper into the forest and saw a jaw-like cave and rested over there.

She left peacefully and happy being the only one who was courageous about the exile. Soon she dozed off. The next morning when she woke up, she decided to eat something and checked her bag twice to remember that she had not packed the sandwich. She realized that her sisters wanted her to die the fate of no food. She was also short of money.

Rose said to her," I do believe that I don't need money or food to survive as there are lots of plantations in this forest." Rose had a family photo with her mother before she was dead. She decided to learn how to survive in the wild. Soon it became 3 years and she was pregnant. She decided she would go to the city. Rose had changed a lot. After all, she no more wore normal dresses, she wore simple jungle dresses. She decided to go to her home and make her child grow up there and then continue her exile. It was a surprising thing that her sisters didn't have a baby but she had one. The previous night she was pale with discomfort and somehow she delivered a baby. Rose changed into her formal clothes even though she started to like nature's costume. She had to cover the infant. She couldn't leave the baby alone and go, after all, it was her child. After several moments of brainstorming, she found feathers and somehow managed to make it into a blanket. She covered the infant with a feather blanket. Then she started her journey to the city. When she returned to her beloved home, her sisters were already married. Lily lived at home with her husband. Well, when Rose knocked at the door, Lily was so surprised and fainted thinking that she would have a heart attack. Her husband rushed towards her and said," What have you done young lady?". "Young lady!" cried Rose "I already have an infant whom I gave birth to yesterday. I can't live in exile with my child, as the baby should know at least why I am in exile and learn lots of things here". "Is that your sister?", asked Lily's husband in surprise." You never told me about your sister and you had put her in exile. Who are you and why do you have to put exile for that young girl?" Lily's husband added. Lily was so shocked and called Orchid. Orchid came over and greeted Rose as though she has never seen her sister forever. Orchid apologized and was forgiven by Rose. Loving her nature, Orchid asked," Dear sister if you have a child, maybe you should come home. We have transferred your belongings to the basement and then she hugged her. Am sorry for supporting Lily. You are truly a loving and kind sister. I wish I hadn't been so rude these days". "Oh! That was not a problem", Rose said with a grin. Lily never knew that her older sister was supporting her younger sister. Orchid had taken Rose to the house. Orchid and Rose were spending most of the time with the infant. They even named the infant Jessica. Meanwhile, Lily was trying to take revenge by kidnapping the child but the child was under the control of Orchid and Rose. After Jessica was 6 years the rich marathon never appeared. They were afraid of what could have happened to their father. Either their father was dead of his age or died in a plane accident. Everyone at the home decided to do rituals for his death. Everyone had peace and now Rose said boldly that she had confessed to her daughter about the exile. Jessica and Rose decided to leave for the forest as they loved the peace and greenery over there. Orchid and her husband were told late at night," We will miss you". After 2 days Rose and Jessica had gone to the forest. Meanwhile, as they were walking further to the jaw cave. Jessica asked Rose," Mom wasn't I born in this forest?". "It is true Jessica, you were born in this forest before even I knew. I decided to take you to the city to teach you something you will need to know in the future", mom said. The mother and the daughter spent a few happy days in the jungle. They jumped over sticky moats, played in the jungle, tended the flowers, and learned about birds and animals. They also made friends with a blackbird. That day after, Mother had taught Jessica to do sculpture work.

Jessica curiously took clay in her hands and wetted it in a bowl and joined the pieces together. Jessica enthusiastically told," I made this sculpture". All she made was a teddy bear. She took her mother's paint and dabbed pink, green, and yellow together. It came like a swirl and it was beautiful. Her mother was busy helping the squirrel to build its nest. Jessica painted and painted and it became grey. She screamed," Mom, the teddy bear came into grey but I want to swirl. "Don't worry", mother said," You can make another one". Angrily Jessica took the wet clay and joined it together as usual. Slowly she made a doll with black eyes, brown hair, red dress, and peach skin. "This has come out so well and neat", mom said. As she said, the black bird swooped down the shoulder and pecked mother affectionally. Jessica asked mom," Can you make soil paint?". "Yes dear! Should I tell you the story of it?", Mother asked. "Yes please!", Jessica replied. Mother added," Once upon a time an early human took a grain of soil that was light brown. Humans took some water and sticky sap from the trees and mixed them with the soil. Then he slowly started painting with his fingers, it soon became like a caveman's art". Jessica said that was a wonderful story. She said while nibbling marshmallows when her mother was asleep, Jessica took a grain of soil with some nature fruits, mixed it, made paint, and then did another masterpiece (sculpture) of a bird. She continued to make more and more. The complete cave was filled with sculptures. The next morning when her mother woke up and realized that Jessica hadn't slept a wink and was simply sculpting some sculptures. "What are those?", Mother asked with curiosity. "Mom, those are sculptures of an animal around the forest. I realized how important it is to keep the cave tidy. Why not keep all those colourful sculptures. So it will be beautiful around the cave". Soon, both of them started getting attached to the dense, deep, and dark forest. It was so beautiful and colourful Thanks to their work and you can see them venturing deep into the forest even now.

Story 13:
The real monster

Pitter–Patter the rain fell on my knees as I sat on the balcony reading Fantastic Beast by J. K. Rowling. Suddenly, a shimmer went through the words, and a dragon and a dazzling golden butterfly flew out of it. The butterfly landed in front of my side. Red invisible ashes came forth and a silver-coated, eager, and enormous dragon with blue eyes. But, I neither spotted it putting its claws on my skin. It groaned, croaked, moaned, cooed, mooed, and a roar to draw my attention. Suddenly, the dragon flared its silver wings around me to keep me dry from the rain. It was invisible! It got annoyed with my behavior and lurked inside the door. It found my printer and sat on it, thinking of it as a rock. The printer turned on and made a strange clicking noise as seven papers were thrown onto the ground. All the papers had two pairs of azure vitreous eyes and tan fangs. Without the knowledge of it, it walked outside to see me gone. I was busy seeing the 'not in the possession of me' pictures. I also noticed another clue 'chalky, muddy footsteps'. Suddenly, an enormous claw grabbed me and spoke in a gibber language. Finally, it showed itself in front of me. I realized that now, no one needed it. But I didn't understand why he was here. He took a silver translator and said," Wanna have fun?". "Yup," I replied and added," I have to complete my social essay that is About the World". The dragon exclaimed," Good! And I am Silver". We finished an intro about ourselves. "I can

H.Yashnashree

make your essay easier. Pack three things, a camera, five papers, and six pencils," said Silver. After I packed my things, they ordered me to climb on his back with the backpack. Then, Silver made us shrink! And ...he pottered utter nonsense and my globe became a real world!!! He placed me on the globe. We traveled to France, Bali, Paris.....and Scotland happily. Silver suddenly dropped me at Haunted Scotland!!!! Why have you brought me here? I screamed. He said," You are my slave now! Dawn broke the next day as I recognized the magical golden spell and sang it. It was very blabber. I woke up gasping for air from my nightmare. Now I understood how a dreadful nightmare could transform into a dazzling adventure. I hope I can bring another spooky tale to all.

The Treasure Trove of Stories and Poems

Story 14:
Why does the stars shine at night?

Once upon a time, in a valley of flowers, there was only one huge star and one huge moon perched up in the sky. The stars were black and merged with the darkness but his forearms were twinkly. His mother the Moon had friends Neptune and Earth. Whenever they came home, Mother Moon would hide baby star, her son and would spend time with them. The only reason she hid the Baby Star in the cupboard was she didn't want her friends to discover that she had a baby. She decided to show them when Father, the Sun comes from his outing.
When she opened the cupboard she would find baby star doing some funny noises which always makes her laugh. One day Mother Moon and Baby Star walked to see Earth. When Mother Moon froze, her light became fainter and paler after seeing the bright sun, talking to Earth. Earth saw Moon and called her to meet Sun. They saw each other in complete silence sh! sh! sh! Because Sun was actually the father of Baby Star! After a while of chatting, Sun came over to their house and saw Baby Star for the first time and hugged him.
Suddenly Baby Star merged with his dad and gave a squish! noise but was finally shiny. Soon, the generation of stars had been coming and so, now we know why the stars have light. The stars also slept and that's why they are healthy and more bright. Now, you kids, sleep then you will become the brightest kid!

The Treasure Trove of Stories and Poems

H.Yashnashree

Story 15:
A Lesson Which A Book Taught Me
(Non-Fiction)

Has a book ever taught you a lesson? It might be a piece of cake to read a book but have you ever observed the lesson in it? Well, I have a book that actually taught me a lesson. One night, I was sitting on my bed reading Harry Potter Part 2 book. The book was absorbed into my brain like a rushing avalanche until it stopped on one page. It was about Harry Potter breaking his arms in the game of Quidditch. I threw the book in frustration. I started fretting about the nightmares of Harry. After a few days, I myself wanted to get back into the book and my anxious mother also told me, "Books might have awful scenes here and there. But the book will be amazing as you read on". I slowly took the book off the shelf and propped down to read the book. As my mother said, It was true the book gave me an awesome adventure of Harry and his friends. Sitting in hatred neither will help. Have any books taught you more than 1 lesson? Well, for me no! But I have also learned one more lesson now do not be choosy about the parts you hate in the book as it will be very interesting further and will always have a happy ending. Why not learn this lesson and read on?

The Treasure Trove of Stories and Poems

Story 16:
The portion that was never told

Ding! Ding! Ding! I rang my cycle bell. How would it be if you were sent to a crowded place? It was a colourful road, with florists blooming flowers everywhere. The thought of the freshly baked croissants, tasty cinnamon rolls, and loaves of bread cherished my parched mouth, but there was a book waiting for me at home. I must keep going, I reminded myself.

As I was ringing the cycle's bell, a plump, cheerful lady poked her head out of the bakery's window. "Howdy!", she chirped cheerfully. She had a greasy, flowery apron covered with all the dish stains and a white dress with blue heart shapes. She was my mother's friend. So, she knew me very well and was the happiest lady on the block. Being my mother's friend, I knew everything about her as well, and she had taught me the direction to the bakery so I could come whenever I liked. Her daughter was in her 20s and was the grumpiest student. She failed to listen to any word from her mother and did the opposite.

The best mishap provided was when her mother had: I told her to buy raspberry jam. But had returned with lard and yam. Her mom told her to buy a packet of chips and a crust. But returned with copper coin rust. Mom told her to buy an apron dress. But returned with a magazine press. This was my favourite poem to sing in the bakery, which her mother used to blush bright red. When I entered the bakery, she was in the heap of bills ticking off lists, and next to her was a packet of flour covering her legs completely. When she saw me, she smiled as sweet as marmalade. "Hello, child! I am busy with a bunch of bills, but what is the treat today?", said Shrirani(my mother's friend). When I handed over the list, she packed it all in a huge cardboard box, and ShriRani smiled and waved me goodbye as I thanked her for the cardboard box. I tied the boxes to the cycle, waving to her," Bye".

I was on my way home when an avalanche of stones hit my bicycle and punctured it. Instantly, the cycle began to fall, and I snatched the cardboard box, wondering what I was going to do now. In the corner of my eye, I saw something sparkling in the sand. It looked more like a gem.

When I tried to pluck it out, vibrant colours washed over it as I dusted it off the sand. When I got it, it was a beautiful hat. It looked more like a classic vintage one. Was it missing? It looked more like a cross between thousands of gemstones and a normal hat.

The hat had a lot of gems sewn on it. Maybe this was the hat that Shrirani lost. That was why she was worried and searching for it. She had not explained the exact reason why she was upset. Carefully but nimbly, I dropped off the box, and my father excitedly ripped open the box that brought out his favourite banana walnut cake while my mother rolled her eyes.

Without telling anybody, I slipped off the bike key and rode back to the bakery, where I presented the hat to ShriRani. I smiled at her and voiced out," Is this yours?". She aired," No, it's not mine". Feeling dejected, I sneaked back home to my room, where I looked more closely at the hat.

I had seen something similar about it somewhere. I leafed through my visual dictionary, but I just found the precious stone that was sewn on the hat. I decided to do more research on that, but I wanted to borrow my mother's laptop when I saw something suspicious on the hat. Feeling suspicious about who would ever forget their own beautiful hat. I felt jokey and put on the hat, and when I saw it in the mirror, I couldn't see myself. Was I invisible? And when I toppled my hat off my head, I was visible again. How was that happening?

I felt like Harry Potter's invisibility cloak. What could I do? Could I give away the hat or keep it? I noticed that on each side of the hat, there was a drawing of fire, earth, water, and air. It was an element. There was something that was etched in French. I was tempted to have my mother's laptop. I heard my mother's footsteps heading towards the mirror on her bedroom wall. She brushed something dusty and pressed the button, making a zip-zapping noise. I couldn't see where she was heading. As soon as I went in, the blaring screen of the laptop hit me. I was about to cut the tab when I saw the invisible hat on the screen. Near that, there was a big sticky note floating up and down.

There was a riddle.

Even the blazing fire
Still, I am to be admired.

Even the thorns of plants
Still, I can grant
Even the drowning oceans
Where darkness motions
Even the cyclones that make you die
Higher into the sky
I cannot be harmed.
But can be charmed.

So that was the riddle etched on the hat. Happily, I rushed out of the room in joy. I had heard that there was a detective shop nearby, so I took my mother's pocket money with her permission but lied to her that I was going to Shrirani's bakery. When I went inside the detective shop, I couldn't help feeling suspicious about my mother. I found a detective kit and bought an ultraviolet gun that was gold in colour.

After buying that, I came home, put on the invisibility hat, and noticed that my mother was trying to lock the door when I slipped into my invisibility hat. Then she went up to the mirror, brought out a violet colour with white shades, and punched a few keys on that. So, that was the dusty object she had. The mirror slid open, and she stepped inside. I followed her suit.

There was a gloomy staircase, and when I stepped inside, the door was shut. I followed my mother and saw that she was going through the hallway full of portraits. She pressed on one landscape, and the stairway led us through. I couldn't help following her. Was I going to be stuck? Or was I going to be buried inside?

Inside the landscape, there was a huge grey platform on which there was a lengthy mahogany table. No one was there, so my mom sat at the very end, taking out a notebook and writing something.

I tiptoed close to her and accidentally knocked over a plastic cup, which fell to the ground. Pitter-pattering to a huge stone, my mother doubtfully looked around swiftly and continued writing. Now I was almost close to keeping the plastic cup. When I tripped over it, I fell, bouncing my leg on the boulder. All at once, the boulder was cut in half and fell into the hole.

I fell and fell and fell and fell and fell and fell as the darkness swallowed me up. There was something so icy as I slipped along the way, and where was I, I wondered? Suddenly, I heard the noise," Mrs. Saluja, it's time for the meeting". In a spark, I heard the commotion of footsteps coming, and they were talking," Mrs. Saluja, have you found the invisible hat?". My Mom replied," No! I don't have it". "Let the meeting end", phrased the chief guest. "And Mrs. Saluja, next time when I meet you, I must see the hat". Soon I tried to get out, but I couldn't.

Suddenly, when everyone left, my mom was alone, looking at the concerned face of the chief, when she decided that she would get back home and learn more about the invisibility hat. She was about to leave when I discussed," Mom". My mother got scared and looked about wondering what the chaos was about. When she noticed something was opening in the boulder, she was terrified that something would happen to me. She didn't know or understand what I was doing there. She used a rope and jumped in. When I took off my hat, my mom saw me and told her truthfully that I was following her. She gazed at me and said," How can you follow me here? It's very dangerous to come here". "What are you doing here", I aired. Mom voiced out," That's nothing according to my timetable. I have Vedantu class". And she awkwardly shuffled out with me. Once we were back in the room, I blurted out," Do you need the invisibility hat?" I closed my mouth guilty that I had told my secret. My mother put it into words," You know what it is?" I stammered," Yup! As I have it". "You have it?", published Mom. I led her to my room, where she gasped at the imaginable but real invisibility hat.

"Woah! How did you get it?", murmured Mom. She was completely out of her head when she saw it. She ran to her bedroom and declared," I have the translator, and she pressed in some keys where the French had turned into English. The same riddle was there and scripted, 'The generation person hat'. It was Shrirani's!!!. Suddenly my doubt expressioned," Mom, I have a doubt. When I asked Shrirani if it was hers, She had replied that it was not hers." Mom stated," That was Shrirani's ancestors who stole it. That is why she didn't know. But that is fine, even though her ancestors stole it. It's proposed as hers". "And by the way, Mom, are you a secret detective?", I asked. Mom said,"Yes," and she smiled.

We happily hugged each other.

H.Yashnashree

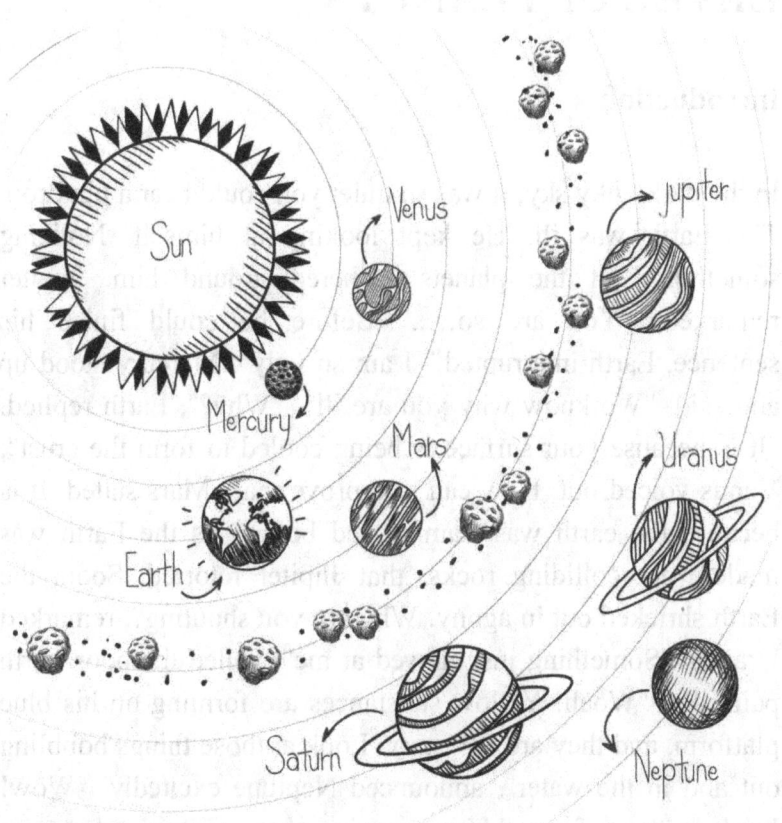

Story 17:
LEVEL UP PLANETS

Introduction

In the dark, inky sky, it was so quiet you could hear a pin drop. The Earth was ill. He kept looking at himself. Noticing something, all the planets gathered around him. Jupiter remarked, "You are so….." Before he could finish his sentence, Earth interrupted," I am so ugly". Mercury stood up and said, "We know why you are ill". "Why?", Earth replied. "It is because your surface is being cooled to form the crust", Venus voiced out. How can you prove that? Mars stated. It is because the earth was flaming red before, as the Earth was made from colliding rocks, that Jupiter retorted. Soon, the Earth shrieked out in agony. Why are you shouting?, remarked Uranus. "Something just clawed at me", yelled the poor Earth painfully. "Woah! Yellow substances are forming on his blue platform, and they are very tiny. Look at those things bobbling out and in the water", announced Neptune excitedly. "Wow! Look at those furry things covering those yellow substances and those giant things around", discussed Saturn. "I think I am getting a new life, said Earth.

H.Yashnashree

Chapter -1: The ...Alien

Soon, life was created, and there was happiness on Earth. After a few days, it was announced that Pluto was a dwarf planet. Everybody started teasing him, as unlike Earth or any other planet, he didn't have life or destruction. Pluto was their best friend, but not now. An unhappy Pluto, sadly, was never seen. Pluto, with his sadness and happiness— a mixture of both emotions very condensed was determined to do some magic. He closed his eyes, determined with courage and wisdom, and neither fought for any of the planets. He went into deep meditation and never woke up. The other planets enjoyed swinging around at full force in their orbits. Suddenly, heard a deafening commotion. Behind them, there was a bullet-shaped thing coming out of the Earth's atmosphere. It was a rocket. The rocket was very loud. It landed on the moon.

The moon shouted, "Get the beetle off". Out came a four-legged thing with a body and a wet nose who kept sticking its tongue out. What was that? Then the creature came up to the planets and uttered, "I am Laika, the first creature to go to space. I am here to understand what is in space. Can you give me a tour around?" Earth smiled at Laika, "I am Earth, the planet that you live on. I am so happy that you are here". "Just a sec", Laika muttered. She just went to fix the rocket, but it blasted onto the moon, and Laika fell and died in grief. Before her last breath, Earth came forward and said, "Thank you, Laika, for coming here. I am the planet of creation, while the others are planets of destruction". Soon, the Earth's humans had become very sad about the death of Laika. Everybody was sorrowful, even the Earth. He got tired of it.

Chapter 2 – The Comet's Tail

One day, the Earth was looking sad when he saw a colourful comet streaking across the sky. It was Halley, the comet. It was his favourite comet, but he was not in the mood as he was dejected. Suddenly, he felt desperate and held the comet's tail. He was being pulled further and further away from the solar system. He loved flying on the comet while riding it. Instantly, a shadow fell on top of him. It caught Earth and was hidden away forever, or not?

Chapter 3- A Ransom Kidnapping but Hidden

The maroon ghost was hidden behind the dark hidden mask. Earth fainted, and when he woke up, he found himself in a pitch-dark prison, and on the top, there was a big hole, but it tightened with asteroids and meteors stuck together to make prison bars. Suddenly, Earth understood where he was. He was in the black hole, the dangerous one. Outside the prison, he saw the Leo star, then the Pegasus star, and a Corvus star. Earth understood immediately. It told him to be courageous as a lion, peace-hearted like a Pegasus, and intelligent as a Corvus. Then came an Orion, and Earth beamed at it. It was a question. It was asking whether Earth had a weapon, but he did not. Again, he looked up, and he saw Orion and Scorpius fighting with each other. Immediately, Hydra came slinking, her tail hanging in the air. The Orion clung to it and was taken high into the air. Up there, he went from cloud to cloud with Scorpius chasing him. Then, with the stamp of his foot, a million stars and Scorpius flew away. Orion was free, and he lived happily ever after. Earth got it.

Chapter 4: The Hugest Mystery

When the masked creature came to the black hole laughing, he said, "How foolish were you? I am the biggest of all, and no one can defeat me". "Jupiter", the Earth thought for a while. Earth studied his features: he was colossal, towering, something so imitating the one who was his best friend, orange effluvia ice kept falling, and whenever he was around, there was something about his super familiar breath. It was a huge mystery related to someone he knew before. When Pluto was a dwarf planet, tears bloomed in his eyes. He was going to have none of his friends back. Soon he stopped being peaceful to get revenge. In acrimony, his eyes turned red with exasperation, and his mouth always tightened in a sour expression. One day, in bitterness, he saw a shooting star, which it eventually boosted up to him, and he howled. I want to be bigger than all the planets in the universe. In a fraction of a second, he swallowed it, and a movement later, in a thunderclap, he burst open and became GIGANTIC!!! Then he became envious of Earth. and planetnapped [kidnapped] him.

Chapter 5: The Furious Duel

"I, Earth, hereby declare you to a duel. Whoever wins will reveal their masks", Earth declared. The suspicious-looking planetage snickered. ''You, you pungy-looking planet, can defeat me?! '' he once again mockingly howled. The masked creature brought out two comets from his back. Earth was not going to give up, even though he did not have any weapons. Earth rummaged through the mud on his lands and brought out a Pachyephalosaur bone and butted it on the masked creature.

The creature shook his limbs for a minute and threw both comets at the Earth. Earth ducked and jumped on the rope that he had seen inside the black hole. He retracted as he flung himself into the galaxies, where the powder made him swirl faster. With the masked creature chasing his tail. Earth, who was drenched in sweat as he rapidly swung and swung with his last chance of breathing, took the dinosaur bone and flunged at the masked creature. Suddenly, the masked creature fell, and his mask came undone. It was an opportunity to see the culprit. Earth held his breath. Straightaway, the enormous figure fell; it was the dwarf planet Pluto. Pluto looks straight into the eyes of the Earth, terrified. The truth had been revealed. In a flash, Earth got up and left, not seeing Pluto's eye contact, who was betrayed by his best friend.

Chapter 6: Humbly, but the Truth "Stop right there."

The sun was up and doing his work. He was a traffic policeman. His sons, the planets, had built their own road, and nobody trespassed on it. The sun had a heated argument with Pluto. "Please show your ticket before you go to my son's house. Pluto stated, "My friendship with Earth is the ticket to life. Can I please enter? I hope that you understand my agony with Earth. We just had a breakup, and now we are both puzzled about what happened with each other". The sun emotionally wiped his tears and said," You can go". Pluto reached Earth's house and revealed that he was jealous of Earth because he had a lot of responsibilities to do and did not care to meet him. They both confessed," Sorry," and their friendship reversed, with the wish of being bigger than Pluto. Friendship is tighter than a band.

....
....

Meanings Constellation – A group of stars.

Pegasus- Horse constellation.

Leo - Lion constellation, one of the brightest stars in the night skies. Corvus- Crow or raven constellation.

Hydra – Hydra, the water snake, is the largest constellation in the night skies.

Scorpius- Scorpion constellation. It is a large star much bigger than the sun.

Orion- Orion, the hunter, is one of the easiest constellations to spot. It is in the shape of an H. Pachyephalosaurs- Dinosaur

H.Yashnashree

Story 18:
One day - One sec

Drip! Drip! Rain splattered on the drowsy city. The orphanage in the city was a hustle and bustle. There was one boy as intelligent as an owl. He was thin and pale, had a huge brain the size of a book, and was always teased about it. Some called him a thin stick or pole. Peter did not mind being teased, he was lonely and had no friends except one. The only friend he had was a baby Chipmunk, which was very cute. Peter had found it one day wounded on the terrace, lying there. Peter had loved to spend time on the terrace of the orphanage, and when he saw the injured Chipmunk lying there, he had pity on it and took care of it. Soon, it became his best friend and companion. That day, when it was raining, Peter sat inside, staring at the window. His chipmunk friend was lying about on the desk, feeling sleepy. Peter himself loved collecting things that had fallen about on the ground; the warden's eye shadow brush, the gardener's drainage pipe, the cook's tin foil, the children's broken toy parts, etc..

Peter put a small handkerchief over his chipmunk friend as a blanket and went over to his small cabinet's closet. Inside, he pulled out a gigantic trunk full of dressing-up playboxes. The warden had given each child a gift such as a discounted kite, a picnic set- tea cups, a Rubik's cube, a dressing-up play box, a furry monster, footballs, wooden bricks, and so on. When Peter got a dressing-up play box, he started playing with it like every ordinary child. He saw it with a fresh pair of eyes. He rummaged through the costumes and brought out a ragged cloak with a wooden stick. He ran into his bathroom and emerged dressed up like a beggar. He brought out a silvery astronaut suit from another. It fit him perfectly. He took out a rag bag and put the costume inside. He himself did not know what he was up to, but all he knew was that he was going to get away from the horrible orphanage. With his chipmunk friend, they splashed over the puddle. Splosh! splosh! splosh! Then the duo went to Chipmunk's house. Inside were water chestnuts, Acron, and areca nuts, which he stashed in the astronaut's suit. Pop! Peter wore the astronaut suit in a second. Near the orphanage was a helipad, there were no people, and what was there was a rusty helicopter leaning against it. Both of them climbed to the helipad and jumped into the rusty helicopter.

Peter didn't know how to use it but had read about it. He turned on the motor and pulled the gear (of course! After wearing the seat belt). The helicopter shot up, and in a spark, Peter lost his balance and was descending. When a rocket blasted up before it could go further, the duo jumped on the rocket head and were flamed higher and higher into the universe. Upon their landing, there was no gravity, and Peter and Chipmunk were floating away. Then all of a sudden the Chipmunk saw a galaxy coming towards them, In fright of floating away, the galaxy was eaten by the Chipmunk, leaving only powder. Seeing that, Peter decided to name her Gala. Gala and Peter jumped onto another galaxy near the moon rover. They buckled the seat belts and were zooming in on the moon. They played with the moon rocks and were about to jump to the next planet when a black hole appeared and sucked them up. Beads of sweat formed on Peter's forehead and POOF!!!!!!!!!!!!!! They were back at the orphanage. There was one moonstone on Peter's hand. Was his dream real or not?

H.Yashnashree

Story 19:
A Special Rescue Centre (essay)

'Grow through what you go through', a symbolization of love and affection, stands in the RESQ animal centre. The health and safety of animals overcomes everything to them. A warm heart lies within them. A rescue centre is what and where a special animal lover's world lies within as the others realize their mistake about endangering or trafficking animals. Lying beneath this world is a huge group named the RESQ in honour of prodigious animals who sacrificed their time to give them well-loved blissfulness for our feathery and furry friends. This RESQ centre in Pune spreads awareness to all the children in urban cities. 10,000 plus animal lives have been saved at the neck of the time. The animal life is in the palm of the RESQ centre, as they do not take a break until they are contented and satisfied that the animals are treated with love and happiness. There was a day when the air of woe surrounded them as they noticed the misery of rabies had started. The whole team got their real weapons out. It was their helpful hands with a box of medicines. Thankfully, the rabies soon passed by, and everything was back to normal. Even the animals that were being suffered from rabies also were helped, and they survived. The release days were heartwarming and wretched days that brought tears to your eyes. The tears are afloat, with a mixture of happiness and sadness unraveling their muddy footsteps as they run or lift to the sky. The glorious moment on which the before the days are numbered before the animals go back to the wild as an experience of happiness that they had at the RESQ centre. The orphaned animals could experience a slight change in being lonely, but they are treated with love and respect. I would like to bring change to the world by making humans love animals. We children would like to make a change in the world as well by Working hard to help the animals.Not misusing the sources.Supporting the RESQ centre with their job. I chose this RESQ centre because they treat animals with so much love and respect. It is special the way the bond grows tighter with the animals. A doctor knew how painful it was for a dog named Hope, who had a train accident. She survived the night once she was back to normal. She was released to a place but used to visit the centre every day. A similar doctor went to work. When she spotted Hope, it sounded like she needed a home. So, the doctor took her into the car and treated her like her pet. You see the actions of the ill-treated animals; people now have a soft heart. Each animal is a source of pride in every way. Some people love hunting in prized collections, so I plead them to assist the facilities.

Story 20:
The courageous girl

Whirr! Whirr! The treading of the bicycle tyre squelched at Heidi's boots. Her naughty twin brother and sister were playing with her father cleaning Heidi's bicycle. Her twin sister's name was Helen and her brother's name was Hector. Helen and Hector were 3 years so they practically did not know what was what. Her father, Harrison was replacing Heidi's tyre. Heidi enjoyed knitting scarves, sweaters, and other items to pass the time. Their grandmom used some huge needles, moreover, Heidi started liking to knit with her grandmom. From that day on, Heidi had a passion for knitting. Furthermore, Heidi loved animals. She had a desire to tame animals in the wild. Heidi slowly stealth away into the shadows. Her mother was sleeping in their bedroom. Heidi tacitly ketchupped the tater tots and furthermost, Golden Sponge Cake with Creamy Filling was buttered with the sourdough. Heidi blanketed her handkerchief and placed it in the hay basket. Heidi slung it over her shoulder with a bottle of hot milk and left home. She skipped gracefully through the golden maize as she came to the clearing, she jumped over the pebbles leading to the river. There she saw a rickety wooden boat. It had green little patches of mosses.

The back of the wood was peeling, making it hard to resemble a boat. But still, Heidi knew that it was a rugged little boat and never gave up hope on that. Heidi clamorously pulled out a medley oar and bounded into the boat and started the boat. Heidi spun the oars and let out a distinguished cry. She was about to reach the land when she lost her footing and fell into the river. Most of all, she was drowning and needed help. She thought of her family as she spat the salty water. She saw a coral reef below. She caught one in her pinky finger and made her way high. But it was not working. Suddenly, she saw a floating stone but not just far behind was the snakehead fish charging towards Heidi. Heidi had an awful feeling about this as she tangled her legs in the coral reef. She pushed one leg down and hit one up. The snake head was coming closer. Fastly, Heidi held the floating stone and jumped up. She landed with one leg on the floating stone and the other on the boat. More and more schools of snakeheads slithered through the water. She jumped on the boat and expeditiously hit the oars. Once she was back safe on land, she rushed home immediately. At home, her mother saw her and was terrified of what had happened to her. Mother began to admit," I am here to confess that you had a long last sister who went out like this only and was killed by a school of snakeheads". Heidi began to cry silently as she brushed her fringe. She looked at the mirror, she had a scar that showed her courage that would last forever.

The Treasure Trove of Stories and Poems

Story 21:
The mysterious adventure

One summer afternoon when the sun was shining brightly, Lakshna, the younger sister, was playing a treasure hunt with Yashna, the middle sister. Suddenly, a delivery guy came to the house and said, "You have three packages". Yashna excitedly called Juana, the elder sister. The three sisters opened the packages. They were three VR headsets for each one of them. Yashna thought it looked stunning. She turned it to the side panel and opened it. There was a keyboard, and she typed 'Dragon World'. After Yashna wore it, suddenly there was fog. There were two dragons who were chasing her. Yashna ran for her life and saw an ice cream shop. She went inside and found a dragon was wearing a butler costume. He looked fit in a white T-shirt, black pants, a green tie, and a badge saying 'John'. He said," What would you like to eat, Madame?". Yashna surveyed the place and replied," I would like to have hot chocolate and a vanilla sundae". The butler said, "Here is the menu". Yashna went through the menu and mumbled, "Seriously, there is nothing a human can eat". The dragon kindly said, "You can trek to a mountain where there is a magical flower, which is an actually for humans. If you eat it, it will be almost like human food". "Thank you so much," she said. Meanwhile, Lakshna took her VR set and typed in a side panel as 'The Coco Melon World." When she went there, she saw a baby called Jiji. Lakshna and Jiji rode Jiji's school bus together. At school, his teacher shook hands with Lakshna, and they did some painting. They painted whatever they wished. Lakshna did finger painting while Jiji did a funny landscape. Meanwhile Juana searched for a racing bike in her VR set. She chose a fire engine bike and started it. There were options for where she could go, so she went to the Dragon World. Juana had fallen in love with the beautiful landscape. In the Dragon World, Yashna was very bored. Looking around, she realized that it could take a day to explore the big world. Suddenly, Juana came in with her fire engine with a big gust of air. Surprised, she asked, "Good lord! Yashna, what are you doing here?" Yashna replied, "I was discovering this new world". "Shall we get a good dessert", proposed Juana. Yashna answered, "When I asked the butler at an ice cream shop for some sundae, he said they only have spicy dishes. There is nothing for a human to eat. Even if there was something fit to eat, we would have to pay them with marbles." Juana said, "Is there any relaxation resort?" Yashna chuckled, "Girl, that is a good idea, but I don't know any resorts here". Juana asked, "Can't we ask butler instead?" "Yeah, but I think we are 5 kilometres away from the ice cream shop". Meanwhile, Lakshna was having fun with Jiji's family. She had a fun time learning at school, and they were having pasta for dinner. Later, they decided to go to the park together. At the park, there was a slide, two monkey bars, four swings, and five seesaws. There was a beautiful garden with many beautiful flowers as well. While Lakshna and Jiji played on the swing, Jiji's brother and sister played on the monkey bar. Jiji's best friend at school, Romeo, played on the slide. In Dragon World, the butler, John helped the sisters by giving them the resort information. He said, "There is a resort that is 20 kilometres away from here. It is too expensive and you should pay 20 marbles." "Thank you", the girls replied. Yashna groaned and said, "Seriously, we are in trouble. Now we need to sell something to get 20 marbles to go to the resort." They plucked some flowers and tied them with a rope, which was actually a creeper. They sold the bouquet to a dragon. He gave them 30 marbles for the beautiful bouquet. The girls were super excited. They went 20 kilometres away and finally saw the resort. It was a luxury skyscraper called Daffodils Resort. They went to the reception. The receptionist said, "Welcome! My name is Tia. Your room will be number 2. Have a great day!". The girls paid, and they loved the ambience of the resort. However, the room was not so good. There were no blankets and the bed was hard. The shower was mostly cold. Both of them went to the resort pool. Juana said," Don't we need a swimsuit?". "The water will be too cold for the dragon," said Yashna. Then they saw some huge waterproof plants. "Maybe", Juana said, "We can make a swimsuit out of that plant". Juana and Yashna pulled out the plant, then cut the leaves out into two swimsuits. At the swimming pool at Scraper 2, when they were done wearing their swimsuits, an old dragon with a grey beard ran into both of them and screamed, "Why did you kill my water plant?". Scared, they both jumped into the water. It wasn't what they were expecting. They had designed the swimming clothes for cold water but it was blazing hot. Just then they saw the signboard saying it was the hot water pool. The cold-water pool was another way. After playing in the water for some more time, they went to their room. They were quite hungry and their tummies were rumbling. When they went downstairs in the elevator, they found it to be very fast. Someone had toyed with the elevator panel and it wasn't an expected ride for them. They felt like throwing up and somehow managed their way to the restaurant. Yashna ordered a cheese pancake but after realising they were out of marbles, she whispered to Juana, "We don't have marbles". The butler overheard their conversation and said, "Do not worry; you don't need to pay. Whatever you order here is included in the amount you paid at the reception. You paid 30 marbles which is 5 extra, so we won't charge you anymore". "Phew! Thank goodness", Yashna said, and Juana ordered a spicy tong soup. Then they happily went upstairs. They knew the food was disgusting, but they didn't know why it was so yummy. Then night fell and both girls took out the VR set from their eyes. Now, they were near their home. Then their grandmom said, "When you went outside, I realized that you were playing with your VR sets, so I followed you wherever you went to keep you safe from the traffic. I was really afraid when you went to the cafeteria, even though you two plucked your grandfather's flowers from the garden and sewed them into nothing, and you tried wearing them also. I made the food and pretended to be a resort keeper because the resort people were saying if you are mad, you are not allowed in, so I made the food. So it tasted yummy. I hope you don't go into any VR dreams. Now your mother is calling you to sleep. By the way, please help me get Lakshna out of the VR set ". The girls pulled Lakshna's VR set out and gave it to the other grandma. The other grandmother said, "Now, I think your mother is calling you to sleep. You all can play with your VR sets tomorrow". Suddenly, Yashna's mom screamed at Yashna and Juana, "What were you thinking? In the evening, you both jumped into the tub full of water which I had kept for Lakshna's shower. You played for so long in the cold water. I think your VR sets are making you crazy". The girls secretly winked at each other and dozed off. The End.

H.Yashnashree

Story 22:
Catfish as mercat (Dialogue writing)

EXT Scene 1: Thunder beaten lake–evening

Screenshot of a weather-beaten lake.

INT Scene 2: Thunder- beaten lake- evening
As the thunder crashes outside the lake. The water ripples inside.

INT Scene 3: Quiet–bright room- evening
A short-haired Yashnashree writes her diary with her newly adopted kitten in hand.

EXT Scene 4: Between roads India- evening
Padma Rao and Priya Patil walk past people. They look very suspicious.
    Priya (Welsh accent)
   "Why do we look so suspicious?"
    Padma (German accent)
   "Dunno"

EXT Scene 5: Thunder- beaten lake–evening
Inside, something is happening, and a glow of light flutters outside the water.

H.Yashnashree

INT Scene 6: Quiet bright room–evening
"Yashna", down-stairs a call fades to her room.

EXT Scene 7: Yashna–house gate- evening
Outside Yashna's house is a van that zooms quickly away from sight.

INT Scene 8: Yashna house- evening
Yashna went down to see and got a shock of life.

INT Scene 9: Yashna house- night
Yashna's parents were gone, and the house was in darkness.

EXT Scene 10: Garden- night
Yashna went out for fresh air and somebody put a gag on her, and she fainted.

EXT Scene 11: Speed off- night
The van with Yashna took off somewhere.

INT Scene 12: Bare cellar- morning
When Yashna came to, she noticed how long the walls were, a hanging bed, and rigid cellars.

EXT Scene 13: Bare cellar–morning
Outside, Yashna heard voices it was coming from below the window.
    Woman -1 (Surprise)
    "You got back Priya?"
    Priya (yawns)
    "Yes! Padma"

She learned the kidnapper's name and brushed her out of the gloomy window to learn more.
EXT Scene 14: Bare cellar–morning
Talking continued….
　Padma
　"She does not have the mercat?"
　Priya
　"Yup,"
INT Scene-15: Bare cellar–morning
There came a muffled noise from up.

INT Scene 16: Bare cellar–morning
There was a boy of Yashna's age and was peeping below a hanging bed beside Yashna.

INT Scene 17: Bare cellar–morning
The boy was unhappy with whipcord as well.

INT Scene 18: Bare cellar–morning
Yashna and the boy's gag were removed by Padma, who came in to, fed us both, who were hungry.

EXT Scene 19: Forest–morning
The window was finally opened and Yashna quickly jumped out without thinking twice.

EXT Scene 20: Forest–afternoon
Yashna grabbed a vine and slid on the lush tree.

EXT Scene 21: Forest–afternoon
Yashna sat and threw the vine to the window.

EXT Scene 22: Forest–afternoon
The boy swung out, scared.

EXT Scene 23: Ground–afternoon
Yashna swung after him, and they landed.

INT Scene 24: Subway- afternoon
Establishing hot of a metallic subway.

INT Scene 25: Subway–afternoon
    Boy (chuckles) (Indian accent)
"You want to know how I am?"
    Yashna (thinks) (Indian accent)
"You were so silent, sure."
The boy removed his shaggy bags and revealed a vaguely familiar tone of voice.

EXT Scene 26: Subway station–evening
    Boy (Gleefully)
"I am Vivekananda, Yashna,"
Vivek was her classmate at school.

Ext Scene 27: Bare cellar–evening
    Padma and Priya were fretting like anything because the children had escaped.
    Padma (scowls)
"She has the mercat and doesn't know what it is."
    Priya (groans)
"Blame yourself"

EXT Scene 28: Subway- evening

Yashna never knew that her classmate was so good at disguises.

 Vivekananda (yawns)
"After one whole hour, we are going home."
 Yashna (growls)
"I can't believe that we are...."

EXT Scene 29: Station–evening
Before Yashna could finish her sentence, Vivek dragged her out and ....
 Vivek (whisper)
"I think that the burly man is Padma's henchman."

EXT Scene 30: Yashna's home–night
Vivek walked with Yashna to her house.

EXT Scene 31: Yashna's house–night
Safely tucked in an aquarium of Yashna's fish for entertainment, her cat was clawing at it. (the fishes).

INT Scene 32: Yashna's house–night (while stroking cat)

 Yashna
"I will name him Fishy."
 Vivek (curiously)
"What was that mercat they were talking about?"
 Yashna
"Dunno"

INT Scene 33: Yashna's house–night
Suddenly, Fishy turned into a cat with a fishtail.

INT Scene 34: Yashna's house–night

Fishy (solemnly) (accent none)
"My real name is Catfish"
Yashna(stammer)
"What?"

EXT Scene 35: Weather-beaten lake–dawn

Catfish
"Could you take me to your nearby lake?"
Yashna
"Sure, do you swim in the water?"
Vivek
"So funny"

EXT Scene 36: Weather-beaten lake–dawn
The group came to the old lake.
Catfish
"You can have three wishes, say them."

Yashna
1. Question 2
2. Take Vivek to his home.
3. Yesterday and today, my parents were missing. I need them.

EXT Scene 37: Weather-beaten lake–dawn
Catfish
"What question?"
Yashna
"Why did Padma and Priya kidnap us, forgetting you? How do they know you are a merkat?"
Catfish

Padma was walking and saw your parents and you were playing with me by the window.
Padma and Priya are twins, who got me as a birthday present. After seeing you with me, they
 felt jealous and…..
　Yashna and Vivek
　　And…?
　　Catfish
And I had revealed that I was a mercat.

EXT Scene 38: Weather-beaten lake–dawn

Awkward silence.

EXT Scene 39: Weather beat lake–dawn
Vivek and Yashna
　　"Bye"
Catfish makes him disappear into his house.

EXT Scene 40: Weather-beaten lake
　　Yashna (hisses)
It is becoming morning fast
　　Catfish
　　　Bye!
　　Yashna
　　　Bye!
As Catfish disappears, Yashna's parents appear and she went home happy.
　　　The End

H.Yashnashree

Story 23:
King Zeus Of Jupiter

"I wonder when the newspaperman arrives", I mumbled to myself. I sat on my new velvety couch, tapping my legs impatiently. Finally, the newspaperman rang the doorbell and slid the newspaper under the door. I ran my fingers along my oak-paneled door, recounting that I was a secret NASA agent and that I had bought my own house. I walked through the veranda to the kitchen and grabbed a plateful of buttered toast and a coffee from the blender. I sat on my couch, had a bite, and read the shocking news in the newspaper. The headline wrote' NASA is going to find a new planet', and down were the respectful names of the people who were going to be participating; down at the last was my name. I excitedly wore my NASA space suit and ran out of town to the NASA center. When I reached our boss, he helped us put on our spacesuits, and we boarded a moonlight-coloured, red laser rocket ready to be launched. I saw a bundle of raw food loaded into the spaceship. Soon, the rocket launched into space, and it took us 2 months to reach space. I was eating raw macaroni and cheese when the rocket shook, I fell out of the window, and everything went black. I felt myself sliding down something invisible. I grasped some stones and heaved myself up. I rubbed my hands and saw King Zeus of Jupiter's dusted statue! I saw our rocket coming searchingly for me! Soon our team trod down to Jupiter, took pictures of the King Zeus statue left on Earth, wrote a dazzling article about the statue, and were very excited to have another new adventure coming up. The next day, I woke up to find a ghost. It was a letter! I peeled it open with curiosity and saw a letter, a pamphlet, and a newspaper. I read all the letters, which bore the same headline: NASA is a failure. As I reached the NASA center, they told me a launch was going to be started. I yelped, "Guys nothing happened. Please be calm". They kept quiet as I raced out. NASA is amazing. Our distinguished boss at NASA has appealed for a glamorous statue on Jupiter that has been structured on its own. The boss says," Our significant worker here, Yashnashree, has done a major from the little mishap". I knew it, my plan was like on a tip of an iceberg. Thanks to my healthy tragedy that found us getting to know the statue.

The Treasure Trove of Stories and Poems

H.Yashnashree

Story 24:
Grief- stricken time

Hoot! Hoot! The nearby branch snapped. A pupilless gleam debuted out through the serpentine trees. A boy in his twenties was chopping out branches from a tree. Hiss! A woman dressed in green with no pupils went to attack him. The boy had natural black hair. His eyes shone like blue. The creepy woman slowly sang a curse song, "Oh, little boy in blue." "Coming in a green hue." "I don't show where I am; it's a small clue." "I skip like dew." "Why did you come to my forest?" "Do not come any closer." "Go back to being evil." (curse) "You little devil" The angry forest guardian stomped away. Meanwhile, the boy turned into a small baby. He crawled to a small den where there was a creek. The baby had the guardian's power so badly that one of his eyes became pupilless like hers. The baby sniffed the air and caught a whiff of trounce. Near to the creek were a pair of chits, like robot parts. The baby touched the robot part with both of his hands because of the raves in his mind.
The flaming parts were touched, and both of his arms fell down. He started weeping. After the accident, his growth from zero months turned into 10 years. In that immediate reaction, he heard something rustling. He lunged forward and hit something ironic. It bruised his forehead, and one of his teeth broke out. It was a pistol pointing upwards. "Hey, it is just a little boy; wait, is he a spy?" Goo Go Ga Ga! What! Gi Gi! The

boy had been amused by the robbers, who then thought of him as a clueless boy. They decided to raise him as their own. They scooped him up and darted all the way to their secret spot. Their secret spot was in a swamp. The pinecone trees wrapped their branches around it, forming a gate. The chestnut trees each had a huge hole at the top, and one of the robbers leaped into it with the baby. It was an old, dusty interior wall made of bark. With the name R.A.T., which stands for robbery and tackling, etched on the bark. One robber slid down the bark, the other used a rope ladder and swung himself to the boss of the committee, and the other robber ran across the pinecone tree branch—the gate. The robber had slid down the bark into a secret tunnel, and only then he had perceived that the boy had no arms. He gazed at the boy intensely, as one of his eyes was pupilless. What a revelation for that appropriate robber who said to himself, "He might be one of the scariest robbers of our community. He will surely highlight our community". Thinking about that, he brushed the boy's blonde hair, but out of his grip, he severely put his hands high, and accidentally, the baby fell down. One more robber was cutting the electrical faults.

When the baby fell, the electrical shock came closer and closer, and the boy's hair became silver. His hair stood up with little ledges like a rock star. At first, his mouth went crooked, then it zipped permanently. Five huge scars appeared on his nose, next to his pupilless eye, neck, ear, and forehead. Every part of the body blistered. The robber named him Roben. Finding out the result of his scary looks they presented him to the CEO. He looked extremely pleased with a heartbreaking figure that could be used to represent his company. First things first, ordered the CEO, "What is his name?". "Sir, it is Roben", said one of the thieves. The CEO waved his hands and said," Go to the laboratory and do something about his hands". The two criminals took Roben to the secret laboratory. One of them snatched a piece of chalk from the cover and started writing formulas on the blackboard. They had a deep discussion about the design, which was finally decided, and they started their progress. It took days and nights to complete the process. The design looked amazing, but when the day and night were done, they noticed Roben suddenly turning 13 years old. His growth was so fast. 13-year-old Roben tied his hand and used the communicable button on his robot arm. He pressed the button to say, "Where is my other arm?". The robbers nervously fiddled with their gadgets when they realized they didn't have very much robot parts to complete the arm. In one week, Roben learned karate skills and was ready to fight. The CEO opened his iPad and showed him their culprit. A scarlet-haired girl with her name,Sydney, written down. Sydney is the most dangerous girl ever conquered. The beautiful girl in the photograph looked pleasant as usual. Roben chuckled," I shall get going to meet her end". Roben was intrigued to go to the city, as he was born in the forest. "He doesn't know the skyscraper's lights or the different smells", muttered the robbers. The CEO was also surprised to know that he could talk. The robbers slyly told their boss that they had inserted a communicable and understanding button in his robot hand. The boss told him," Where is your other hand?". Roben countered," Our army did not build my another hand, but I am still glad to be freakish". The boss pressed one of the buttons that swallowed the city map inside him. One of the robbers held his hands up and asked," I wonder if he will need a disguise"."Yes, he does", said the boss. The robbers pushed open the door and took Roben inside. First, they smothered his silver hair and buckled him in a blonde wig. They pushed the bangs near his pupilless eye and gave him a brown dress. Meanwhile, he noticed a pink shimmer, and that was when he started liking pink. He also noticed a wooden flute that was lying in the corner. Roben picked it up and pressed it to his lip straight away, and music started flowing out. Three times, he loved to play the flute. The robbers dressed him up as a musician, but they could not do anything for the robot hand. They had to let him go like that. Roben had to rush to the forest. He was on his way when the guardian of the forest was thinking about him and went into his future. It was such a nuisance that she decided to do something about it. She touched the bark of the wooden trees, and amber spilled on her soft hands. She collected some leaves and branches to form a triangular shape, and she filled the amber inside it. Then she went up to the rainbow and collected a glitz of string. She tied the dollar to it and was extremely pleased. She cleared her mind by thinking of that as a life-ending necklace. She cleared her mind of the emotions and located him in the forest. She could see him in disguise. Then, swiftly, she opened her eyes and landed at her destination.

Meanwhile, in the presence of the guardian, he started feeling hot, poked with fear, and sweat dripping down the shadows. Instantly, the guardian appeared in his head and boomed," There is a life necklace that you will have to wear. The caution is that you must not remove it.'' Lo and behold! The necklace appeared at his feet. He picked it up and wore it. He continued his journey to his city. He had to cross many sweet birds, but he was in a rage, so he had to keep on imitating it with mock ferocity. Soon, reaching the city was a bizarre type of bliss. On spur of moment, he spotted a flash, and out of it came a girl with fiery red hair that tumbled to her knees. He found out that she could apparate. She concentrated hard as a guy sprinting across the street was muscular with a pizza delivery shirt on. He twirled and found himself in his hero shirt. Roben pulled out his robot hand and pressed a button. A blast shot out and hit their feet. "That is a warning shot, and may it be your end", he cackled. He cantered towards Sydney. He shot another flame. Sydney dodged it and fired her shot, but suddenly he gave her a flaming wok that surrounded her. She felt helpless while her friend, who was also a hero, ran behind Roben and pulled at his neck. At that moment, his wig fell down and showed his silvery hair and pupilless eye. His scars showed his scary looks. Suddenly, Sydney got a light bulb that frenzied. Right away, she started weeping so loudly that Roben took pity on her and her charming looks. Leaving the other hero, Roben pressed the button so that water splashed on all the fires. Sydney started feeling the same hot white-pocked fear through her. The Guardian appeared in her mind, verbalising, " See that amber necklace? His life is stored in that. Snatch it away." Sydney took the advice and got up. She brushed the dust off her hands, pretending to yawn. She moved slowly forward and……snatched the necklace. It snapped into half, and Roben died instantly. Soon the town was saved, and people lived peaceful lives.

The Treasure Trove of Stories and Poems

PLANET BOOK

Story 25:
I have been stranded on a new planet

Chapter 1: Meeting the Characters

The black sky, the galaxies, the children... Wait! What was I doing here? Yup! I remember now. I wasn't shooting off a rocket into space. I was having a swimming competition in the ocean, and suddenly something pulled me, and then somehow I entered the mystical cosmos. I had landed on a phenomenal planet. It had a ring of trinkets. Hold on! This was not Saturn. I had memorized the solar system book completely. The color of this unique planet was a prime rose mixed with lavender and yellow. I murmured to myself, "Wasn't Saturn black and brown? Where have I ended up?" Suddenly, a preternatural, nerve-racking, haunting, eerie noise made it unsettling and anxious in my mind. It was a fleece and fluffy lamb, which was white as a fluffy cloud. A lamb! I splurted in astonishment as a 13-year-old girl popped out in a corner. Ahh! I choked. It is the girl from... "Agatha Oddly, what are you doing here?", I yammered. Agatha said," Don't you know, this is Bookworm Planet, where the best book readers come to our planet to see young authors". "WOW!", I screamed. "Agathaaaa", I ran behind her, "Whose lamb is this?". Agatha rolled her eyes, "This is Suppandi's pet lamb from his pet shop". "Hurray", I yelled as I picked up the soft lamb. Agatha bounced over a crater and jumped inside it. Agatha urged her into the crater. I hopped inside to see Liam Lau digging something into a small hole. Agatha explained that they were searching for some treasure for fun."Bye", said both teenagers as they helped me climb out of the crater. It wasn't much fun walking without somebody who could help me. I stopped to watch a rainbow-coloured pet shop in which Suppandi was trying clumsily to stop the fawns screeching, the rabbits gnawing, the lambs chasing their tails, and some cats who were scratching the aquarium full of fishes. I ran into the pet shop with the lamb and said, "Suppandi, I guess you lost this lamb"." Oh! Thank you", Suppandi yelled on top of the noise," I guess I should thank you with a gift". "You can have this chips packet", he added. "No thank you", I pleaded,"Could I have your autograph? ". Suppandi said," Do you want that drawing, the graph of an auto? ". "No", I chuckled as I rolled out of the shop with amusement. "I know, I wondered, there is no such thing as shops on a planet other than Earth, but what if there was? I was halfway through a landslide when I bumped into Benjamin. He was terrified. He looked up at me and said, "You are the new person coming to our land". I didn't hear who said it until I saw it was Benjamin. I was so excited and asked him, "Where do you live?". He replied," Never mind". I scurried off. I started walking towards the dragon. He was studying a map. Behind him, there were four dragons. I ran forward to see that they were vaguely familiar. In excitement, I speeded up to Dragonets. They were from the Wings of Fire, named Glory, Tsunami, Clay, Sunny, and Starflight. They showed me the map and told me where to go, and I thanked them with pleasure.

Chapter 2: Rainbow Outfits

I may not notice, but this planet was so beautiful with endless rainbows and colorful shops, and I wondered if I could use a helicopter to see above the world. It would look like a colorful doll set for my sister. There were lush pet animals, and their clothing was unique. I was dying to have a journal to write about this trip. I bumped into Suppandi, who was trying to catch his lamb, and I said to him," Ciao! What is your traditional outfit?". But he wasn't in the mood to listen. So I ran past him, sat behind a stone, and recorded in my mind that these people had unique clothing. Some people, like Suppandi, wore a normal red shirt and white shorts that resembled the red color in the rainbow as love (Starflight had told me about this informative and respectful people's color coding). Agatha and her friend wore orange overalls that represent intelligence. Dragonets like Sunny had yellow scales that represented happiness. Glory had green scales that represented quirky camouflage. Tsunami, which had blue scales that showed the victorious. Benjamin wore indigo tops, which meant creativity. Clay had brown scales that showed strength, and the black scales of Starflight represented inspiration.

Chapter 3: Cultural Habitats in the Role

Bookworm Planet had an intriguing habit of making crafts such as origami birds, folding them neatly, and writing notes inside them. Throwing them high into the air so people can catch them. The bound book was on paper, and the pages were glossy. They were very good at medicine and healing. I dreamed about those when I tripped on a huge, sharp stone and fell. The blood was oozing out, and I wanted more about this planet, but my leg was desperate for a rest. Agatha found me lying on the floor and said," You, what are you doing here?". I showed her the bruise on my knee. She said," Wait here! I will get you some medicine". Meanwhile, as usual, the soft lamb was still running with Suppandi behind his tail. I caught the warm lamb and handed it over to Suppandi. He laughed and said, "Thank you." Pets have not gone through the market for sale, so I would like to thank you for giving me a lamb or a pet. No wonder I already have two chickens at home. "It's okay", urged Suppandi, and gave me the lamb. I was so happy, I asked," Do I have to pay you?". "Sure", Suppandi said. Suddenly Agatha replied from behind," Suppandi, I will give you the money for the lamb" and paid him. The lamb baa..aaa, as it trotted next to me. Agatha declared, "I have got the medicine. Suppandi, step aside". She applied an invigorating, cool paste that looked like sandalwood. I asked Agatha curiously," What do you eat?". "We eat a hazelnut that we cut into half, inside creamy, snowy, that is whipped into a dollop that has been inserted with an edible golden miniature book that has vanilla semi-glossed pages. The mini-book has write-ups about how good-hearted a person should be. If you eat it with a good heart, you will become intelligent and kind-hearted", Agatha added." Wow", I aahed. My lamb bleated for a moment. I almost forgot about its presence. Starflight was nearby and showed me a folder that he made. The texture was very slick, and inside were several files gagged together. I picked up one of them. There were some pictures of him and the Dragonets of Destiny with Harry Potter. There was a graph chart showing the number of times each one of them learned how to memorize the map of the bookworm planet, and there was a map and some secret drawings he had done. Starflight gave a smug smile and folded the files. Agatha spoke up,"

Would you want to learn more about our planet?" "I love to",I chirped.

Chapter 4: Twist

Instead of Earth, which had green and brown trees, after you eat this tasty, unique kind of food, the book will be planted. The books emerged from the soil that was stacked neatly. Instead of a tree, it was a book tree, and their food grew on it. There were no such things as grounds, and it is glass that is fragile. Suddenly, Clay, who was having battle training, swooped his tail on my spine. I fell on the huge boulder, gasping for air. The boulder cracked into two. There was a rainbow glow that stopped, and a species that was a combination of sheep, lions, scorpions, and deer arose from the shadows. "Wow", said everyone in agast. Suppandi's rare collection was this beast. I asked an unexpected question," How can I go home?". Benjamin jumped up and said," I know, read a bedtime story, and you shall go to your land". After reading the bedtime story, I found myself drowning in the water. Suddenly, they placed something huge on my chest that clanged. It was a medal. When I opened my eyes, I saw my first-place medal and told my parents seriously," I have swum with my eyes closed, and I don't know what happened". My mother giggled and said," Don't be silly". "Okay, if you believe so", I told them. They hugged me. As I came home, I was holding something in my hand. It was a small golden book with pictures of my adventures with them. The fawn and lamb were small golden statues that were given to me, as they couldn't accompany me.

The Treasure Trove of Stories and Poems

H.Yashnashree

Story 26:
The longest badminton shot

Chapter 1: Introduction

"Yashna! How long are you taking?" said Mom from the kitchen. "Mom, I won't take so long", Yashna groaned. Yashna had gone to get a pair of socks for her badminton class. As soon as she got it, she scampered down the stairs and placed it in her bag. Mom shouted, "I am starting the scooter, come fast". Yashna sighed, heaved the bags and dashed through the garden. Her pet roosters, Sunshine and Meadow, bounded after her while she playfully nudged both of them in the side of their tails. As soon as she reached the gate, the roosters skidded themselves to a halt and put on a goodbye expression on their faces.

Mom closed the gate and hopped on the scooter, with Yashna also perched behind her. Then they speeded through the roads to their destination, Yashna's badminton class. "Bye!", Yashna and Mom said together as Yashna got down at the gate of the badminton center. She ran gleefully toward the center and stopped at the building with yellow and red bricks. Yashna absent-mindedly chewed her nail as thousands of thoughts buzzed around her like a honeybee. She wondered if Brithi, Shestra, Adhifa, and Sahastra would come because they never came for the holidays. It was troubling her that her friends might have left the center, or maybe were still on holiday.

Yashna took a deep breath, stepped into the center and ran up the stairs. She was on the last and topmost floor where her badminton class took place. She stared into the empty corridor and saw a shadow looming across the wooden steps. A girl with a dark bob standing near the bench. As the lights were off, she couldn't see who it was. Suddenly, it appeared to her that it could be Brithi. "Brithi?", Yashna called out. "Huh!", Brithi replied. Yashna reached out and turned on the light switches. Finally, she could see everything with the lights on. She saw Brithi standing near the wooden steps, vaguely distracted twirling her hair. Her gaze fell upon Yashna worriedly, and she ran towards Yashna with arms wide open. Yashna asked Brithi, "What happened?". Brithi said, "You might not know this but Shestra, Adhifa, and Sahastra, you and I are partners but since Shestra and Adhifa haven't yet started their classes because of the holidays Sahastra, you and I will be partners".

Yashna tried to lighten up Brithi's mood and asked, "What's the problem with that?". Brithi uneasily hesitated for a moment and replied," Sahastra and I have enrolled you in the longest badminton shot of the year contest because I can't do it as I sprained my leg and Sahastra can't do it,". She added, "Some man was walking with a clipboard in his hand, walking towards each of the partners, and we were made to enroll at least one for the contest". Yashna's face became pale and their jaws opened. "So you have enrolled me in the competition", said Yashna in disbelief. Brithi fidgeted and groaned,"Ya" and she added," I have booked these two courts for us today for practising". Suddenly Sahastra zipped up and said," Hello guys" and her gaze fell on Yashna, and she too became quiet. "Ya, I know, I know", moaned Yashna, "You think I am cross with you". Sahastra nodded shyly at Yashna. Yashna saw

Sahastra was holding a primrose-coloured bag labeled for Yashna. Brithi nodded towards the bag and joked, "I wonder what she stored in it for you today". Sahastra pulled out a pair of lavender sneakers, white lace socks, and a box of shuttles. There was a small, awkward silence. Brithi broke the ice and remarked, "Hope there is no fancy parade coming yet". Soon, they finished their warm-up exercises and Yashna practised her best to smash it to the back box of the court. Indeed, it didn't go any further. Yashna was disappointed, took her gifts, and went home. Her friends followed her and left for their respective homes.

Chapter 2 :The Greatest Advice

Yashna was preoccupied with the thoughts of the longest shot of badminton of the year. As her teacher started writing on the chalkboard, her best friend, Manya, smiled goofily and tapped Yashna on the back. "Yashna", Manya whispered. "What are you dreaming about?" Yashna spoke in a low-pitched voice, "I have no idea. I don't feel interested in hearing about the subject". Manya replied, "Actually, you must be attached to listening to a particular subject because doing what you love makes you feel inspired". "Yes, I think you are right", Yashna said. Later, she walked to her badminton class, thinking about Manya's advice. Suddenly, she felt inspired and had an urge to do something immediately. When she reached the badminton court, her friends greeted her and Yashna shared her plan with them. She whispered, "Brithi, buy a four-length rope, and Sahastra get a huge rock from downstairs. I will do my stretching work". Sahastra walked to Kittur Rani Chennamma Stadium and saw a huge boulder towering before her. She tried to carry it, but it didn't work. She ran back to Yashna and asked her for help. Yashna told her to get a medium-sized rock.

Finally, Sahastra got one and placed it before Yashna. Yashna uttered, "Thank you". Brithi walked in with a huge cardboard box and blurted, "The shopkeeper from whom I had bought this rope gave me a free trampoline, which is too small and on which only babies can fit". Yashna remarked, "Wonderful and useful. You guys all watch me". Yashna tied half of the rope to the boulder and the other half to her hips. She asked Brithi and Sahastra to keep the trampoline near the boulder.

Yashna leaped on the trampoline, did a somersault, a cartwheel, and a little twirl in the air, and landed perfectly on her feet. She said, "This is how I am going to practise for the longest badminton shot. I will get the moves correctly". Awestruck, Brithi and Sahastra rolled their eyes.

Chapter -3: Surprise party for the cheerleading

While Yashna was practising, Sahastra and Brithi sat in the stalls and talked about something important: HOW TO ENCOURAGE YASHNA AND CHEER LEAD IN HER HONOUR. Sahastra voiced out, "Maybe we can design cheerleading outfits and accessories. I think we can shop for some accessories". Brithi nodded, "Yup! I remember we discussed this last night. I have got the pocket money". Sahastra darted up and said to Yashna, "Our mother told us to buy grocery from the market. We will come back soon". Yashna kicked up a "Yes " in the air. The two girls scampered outside the block to a shop called Cheerleading Unique. Inside the shop, each aisle was filled with colourful cheerleading stuff. Sahastra hopped in delight to a corner nook of the shop where the aisles were filled in with red-coloured bracelets with medium-sized flashy stones crusted on them. Brithi pushed the trolley to where Sahastra was standing. Sahastra dropped two of the red-coloured bracelets into the trolley.

Brithi beamed with happiness. "OMG! I have been dreaming of buying this stuff". It was 'just a girl who loves cheerleading' pouch. In went to of them in the trolley. Next they scooted with the trolley to the pom-pom section. They selected one pair of pink pom-poms and gold, blue, and white mixed pom-poms. They also took one pair each of metallic pom-poms, a blue cheerleading bow holder, a pink cheerleading bottle, door flexibility, a stretching leg strap, two pairs of outfits, colourful bows, thick bam-bams, and a cheer charm bracelet. Brithi finally paid and swung their shopping bags around happily. Sahastra said loudly," I think we must see YouTube for the cheerleading session". The shopkeeper, Mrs. Rani, asked kindly to Sahastra and Brithi, "Would you like to have a cheerleading session here from 5:00 to 6:00 pm?" "Sure", the girls replied excitedly. They registered themselves for the batch and joyfully ran off to the stadium. Yashna greeted them and said," I have practised how to do the gymnastics for jumping and hitting, and must say, it's going well. Tomorrow is the match, and I am ready. I will have one more practise from 6:00 to 7:00 pm in the badminton court". Yashna left the court, flexing her fingers excitedly for the big day. Sahastra and Brithi called Mrs. Rani for the session. Yashna wondered what was going on between them because they were silent. After Yashna left, Mrs. Rani emerged from the shadows who was listening keenly to the conversation.

Chapter-4: The racking session

Mrs. Rani dazzled as she tapped her chin thoughtfully. She was wearing a hot pink cheerleading outfit with golden buckles and a small badge pinned to her that said First Prize in Gymnastics. A pink ribbon with twirls dangled on each side from Mrs. Rani's beige ponytail, which reached almost to her legs. She looked like Rapunzel in a fantasy tale. Mrs. Rani did the hook-tail dance and the tango dance. Suddenly, Sahastra stopped at one dance and again asked question that annoyed Mrs. Rani: "When are we going to learn the twirl dance". Mrs. Rani picked up her dark-rimmed spectacles and wiped them before wearing them. "Ahh", her voice cracked, "You girls must learn it if you want to". The girls finally learned how to somersault, cartwheel, twirl in the air, and do the tippy-top dance just like real cheerleaders. Soon, the moon came out and showed its silvery, raspy light. The girls sat on the bleachers and chugged water. They huffed and puffed their way home.

Chapter 5: The Fantastic Match Winner Is ...

The next day's dawn broke out, shining its happy light all over the town. Do Re Mi Fa So La Ti To Ti La So Fa Mi Re Do. The VIP's guest room has been blasted with dame Aadarshini, a talented lady in Piano and famous for her classical music. She was sitting in the badminton VIP room, having heat waves all over her face and sweating because of her fur coat. She had an ancient golden gramophone. She was using her grand black slick piano, in turn, to compose a song for the winner. Panchajanya Court had a VIP room, especially down below the earth. It was a secret compartment that nobody knew about, so the VIPs could hide safely without being pounded for autographs until the competition was on hold. Yashna was about to enter the court when she realised it was closed due to preparation. So she called her father through her smartwatch. It was like her own miniphone. Her father had requested his playmate's badminton court for Yashna to play with him. Her father was passionate about playing badminton and was full of beans to hear that she had taken part in the longest badminton shot. Suddenly, a voice screamed in the mike," Hi Yashna". Of course! It was her cousin.

They didn't have their smartphones yet. So they were using their dad's phone to communicate with her. She cut the call. Yashna's father asked her if she could show him her precious smash moves. Yashna blabbered," Sorry Dad, you can watch me perform at the show. If that is the case." He sighed," Okay". After a few hours of private practise in her bedroom, Yashna got ready and rushed to the badminton court with her parents and relatives. They all got seated on the bleachers. Yashna couldn't help but she was proud and filled with pride. After all, the court was made up of green, blue, grey, brown, and black. But now they have decorated from down to up with colourful ribbons, bows, streamers, confetti, and sprinkles. She could not find Brithi or Sahastra, but only their families. Suddenly, her coach was in a slick black outfit with oiled hair and a mustache, in a white vest with a red bow.

He shrugged at his audience. "First, let's have H. Yashnashree on the court to do a smash with her opponent chosen by other badminton classes, and who hits the shuttle to the backcourt or anywhere from two courts miles away will win. They will be selected for the final round, and the winner will get the trophy." Yashnashree came with her racquet, nervously fidgeting from side to side. Her coach remarked, "Yashna will play from team A; Bindhu from team B; Zahora from team C; Diya from team D" After Panchajanya's coach had finished talking about the teams, He yelled," Well, we may begin the competition. Teams A and B are going to show their smash skills". Yashna and Bindhu walked up to the court with their parents, who looked very concerned about the match. Bindhu served the shuttle, and Yashna twirled, somersaulted, and hit a perfect smash. It went overhead as Bindhu crossed the other two courts and landed in the exercise box. Everyone gasped in agast. The coach uttered,"Now, team C and D are going to perform their skills." Zahora and Diya played, and Diya won. It was the time for the final smash. Yashna and Diya were ready to play. Yashna used her rigorous smash, and suddenly, Diya gave her double the challenging smash. Instantly, Brithi and Sahastra popped out of their secret location with the cheerleading outfits and accessories. Yashna lost her footing and almost fell. At once, she held her racket high and kept her hand on the ground, giving her a challenging smash. The winner was Yashna. She held the trophy splendidly. Meanwhile, Brithi and Sahastra shyly used their equipment. Yashna swiftly went to see Brithi and Sahastra wearing one ponytail for the first time. The two girls did hippy dance movements backward. Brithi flung Sahastra on her shoulder, and they did the twirl dance. The day ended happily as the two girls entertained everybody with cheerleading techniques.

H.Yashnashree

Story 27:
The Detective Agent

"Agent Calista Purity, report to the office!!!!", the loudspeaker exclaimed. Calista was a long, wavy, blonde-haired woman. She had blue eyes. She was the top agent crime finder in her community. Whenever there was a case that was out of her hands, they would always depend on her. She raced away to their secret boss's office. When she entered, her boss was relieved. She showed her slideshow and said," I am afraid to say that every cattle is orating from being visible around the world, along with farmer Melissa.'' Calista nodded, but her phone buzzed. She swiftly took a peek at whatever it was. A fashion photo was sent by her best friend, Verity. Being in a bad mood, she switched it off. She saluted to the boss and walked out. Once she was out, she instantly saw something that caught her eye in the fashion photo. Verity was a photographer allowed to send pictures of cultural things. Calista saw that the fashion runway person was……MELISSA?!!! Something was not right about the dress she was wearing. Immediately, she sprinted to the boss's office. When she opened the door to the boss's office, the boss was talking on her phone. Calista caught a few words they were talking about. "It seemed like that was such a hard day, and we actually fooled them, Melissa", the boss spoke on the phone. She found Calista gaping at her in shock. Calista immediately lunged at her boss and snatched the phone, and then there was a deadly chase between both of them. Calista was known the best for her mimicry of voices, too. She harangued in her boss's voice, "Melissa, where is your location? I think I must have forgotten it, please, as all my agencies are harassing me today." Melissa shook her head and made her voice wobbly. "Sure, I can send it unless you keep it a secret", Melissa said. At once, Calista called for backup, and they followed her to the secret location. When they arrived, it was dingy and damp. Melissa had her back turned on a sack of potato chips. "Verity,!!!!!! Are you part of this group? Callista raged. Callista's boss was on this team, and so was her best friend! That could only mean something………. So, all her cases and crimes were fake???. She tried to clear her thoughts away so that she could focus on what was going on. Her backup team was armed dangerously with chains and swung the handcuffs around it. Calista pointed her hand at them, and they all charged with their handcuffs. They all managed to put them in prison, but there was one question still on her mind……………….. She was wondering if she, as the newly elected boss, still had their ex-boss's gadgets. Should that be thrown out or what????……….Later, as she got the newspaper, there was a headline ''ARRESTMENT BUT STILL A FASHIONISTA'' She brought out the fashion picture from her phone and studied it very naïvely. The fur coat was unusual……………… Instantly, it hit her. The fur coat was black and white, which meant the gang that was locked up actually killed the cattle and made them into fur coats. She was so ineffable that she solved one and started to research another for her team………………

The Treasure Trove of Stories and Poems

H.Yashnashree

Story 28:
Let the cat out of the bag

The doorbell rang so loudly that no one could stop it. It was my younger sister at the door, in a complete mess. She always makes herself humiliated by the public in such a hot mess. The reason she makes herself dirty is when she gets a genius idea. Now you are wondering: What's garbage going to do with a genius idea? Let me explain why my sister likes recycling everything in the garbage. Like her toy box was very stained, so we decided to throw it away. She begged us not to throw it away. She locked herself in her room and stayed there for 3 hours. We thought she might be crying. She emerged a while later, looking cheerful. Her expression made me curious. I helped her bring out some kind of recycled thing. She pressed on each button, on which each different type of candy fell on a bowl. We realized she really liked recycling. She turned a medium ball into a fuzzy clown-type monster; she used a pattern block to make a portrait. She used to use the pattern blocks when she was a baby. Out of her soccer ball, she made a globe, and using her sock, she made her own hand-knitted gloves. She was very creative in her recycling. She even made a club called 'Recycle the Beauty, Reuse the Earth, and Reduce the Harmful Pollution'. One bright morning.......okay, evening, when my sister came in with rubbish everywhere, I realized immediately what had happened. This was not her usual plump, happy face. She was crying when I peeked out of the door, and I was figured out that my instinct was right. She had actually rummaged through the dustbin like a raccoon, but she had not ascertained that her friends were looking at her. My younger sister broke down. She elucidated," I was searching in the dustbin because I saw someone throw something. It looked like gold, which I hadn't noticed. My friends were there, and I was searching through the dustbin when one of them pushed me into it and started calling me a rubbish rummager and such things like that. Then I forced myself to let the cat out of the bag about her obsession with recycling things. Nobody believes me now and never knew that my case of obsession was going out of hand". My parents and I pleaded with her to go to school, but sadly, she never listened. She almost missed her classes and refused to go to school. Instantly, an idea struck my mind. The next few afternoons, I called upon myself to get my hands dirty in the garbage, brought a pair of stained gloves, and flicked a video. It started with me taking the gloves inside my younger sister's room, where she made them into a blowing toy puppet, and when I sent her friends the video, they started thinking that it was unbelievably awesome that it converted dirty into useful. Soon, they all rejoined being her friends again.

H.Yashnashree

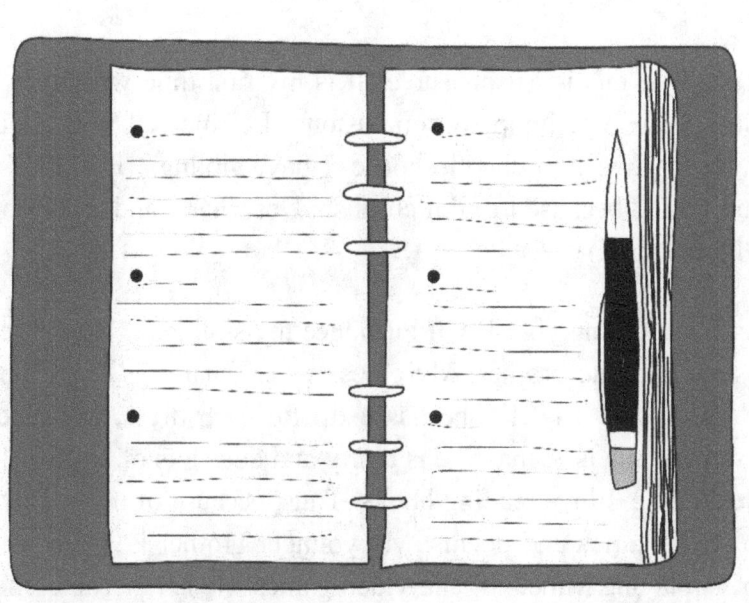

Story 29:
Dear Diary

25-11-2023

Hey guys, this is Yashnashree! It is my first time writing in a diary. Let's not jump to conclusions. Let me tell you about myself. I live in a chaotic house. I have siblings (P.S. Please don't mind because I find it childish: Dear diary, and at the end with my sign.)

As I was telling you, I will introduce my siblings. I have three sisters and one brother. My eldest sister's name is Esha. She loves dresses a lot!!! She has a tip for each dress. My elder sister's name is Juana. She is crafty and does lots of craftwork. Next is me. I love reading books. Thus, because of them, I like to write stories and poems. My younger brother is Vian, who loves playing Minecraft and video games. He is taller than me. My youngest sister is Lakshnashree, who is sweet but naughty.

I had never imagined having four siblings. We had a villa near the sea cove (an area around the sea). When we visited them before, it was a noisy area full of seagulls and palm trees, which whispered to each other in the wind. Now, as we went there, the seagulls did not caw a bit and were friendly to everyone.

H.Yashnashree

We felt relaxed as my mom roasted the pizza; everyone found the corner to entertain themselves. We had a small bookshelf filled with various poems and stories. I was reading Shakespeare's poetry from a global anthology of poems.

I had almost finished it when my mom called me and my family to have food. On the table, there was pizza, and our mom gave us cola, fruits, cheese chips, peppermint, and candies. With the pizza, we feasted on every bit as a combination.

Then my parents let us go swimming in our indoor pool, and after removing our swimsuits and getting dressed up in our PJs, we went down; me, Juana, Esha, Vian and our parents were watching a cartoon. We had fun and experienced a good time. But I felt bad for the younger ones, as they could not see the cartoon.

Good night. See you tomorrow, dear diary.

27-11-2023

Today, we had gone splashing in the green and blue sea, and I was deliberately wadding my feet when a tin can came sliding to my feet from the sea. Inside, there was a soft bed of hay that belonged to a hamster. The hamster peeked out with big blue eyes as if it wanted to go back, gliding through the sea again.

We brought him home and took care of him. He immediately felt home sick, as he wanted to be with somebody at sea. That night, I was intrigued to see the hamster's behaviour and went out and set myself on the sand.

At midnight, as I sat there on the wet sand, the aggressive-thinking hamster looked into the vast sea and curled up into a ball, feeling warm and safe. He liked the vast sea crashing around him. Soon, with him, I went back inside. I guess he started thinking about his past story. Me and my brother always say that rodents are allergic to water, but how come this particular rodent loved the sea? We found it interesting; before I had thrown the tin out, I had found a small piece of paper on the hamster's bed.

It was a year ago, as it was an aged photograph with the dust having an admiral and captain holding the hamster.

I feel sleepy now. I am going to bed.

Bye for now....

29-11-2023

Good morning. All of us were wondering how a hamster could travel in the sea without food. He must be starving, but I was imagining that the hamster loved the sea, and maybe, just maybe, their ship had drowned, and the first thing the hamster did was slide into a polluting tin can.

Was pollution saving this hamster? The other crew members were in the photo, and most of them were slaves. It was a colourful picture.

Now, I will complete my breakfast before coming to write to you.

H.Yashnashree

X-X-X-X-X-X

As you can notice, I am shaking wetly on this phone. Let me tell you that whatever conclusions the little girl has drawn in her diary are true. You might be thinking that I am a stranger. I think I should have a fine for trespassing. I am Leo, the hamster. Okay! I am literally not writing, but getting it recorded on my phone(I am used to it). You might be racking your brain about how I can speak. But in reality, there is a translator on the phone for any kind of creature. As I am telling you, even I got inspired to write a diary. I was having a lot of questions on coming to this house. I was unable to trust this house. I thought that they could be utilizing me for something, but they were gentle with me. I felt a little distrustful for not telling them who I was. I always felt awful for everything, and how could I say that I didn't belong here? I felt homesick and wanted to go back to the sea to curl up. Would they leave me out in the beautiful, clear water? But sadly, I was not sure if they would leave me out.

I wanted to escape by finding a hole to get away from this grisly place. There were other questions in my mind, and I wanted to find out how each thing worked. I was confused, dazed, and had a mercurial mind. I wanted Captain Caleb and Tony, the admiral, with me. I wished I could have them here to comfort me. In my wild dreams, they would never appear, as I loved them so much, but my heart beated hard and said that they were all dead and I had to leave them alone. I now say bye to you diary. As you know, I cannot sign this page as the pen is bigger than me.

X-X-X-X

The Treasure Trove of Stories and Poems

1-12-2023

Hey guys, there is a mystery at home, and I was unable to write as I was busy reading Leo, the hamster's note, on my mom's phone. We did not know it had such a brilliant brain to write a diary note. We were all stunned and wondering how this could have happened, but lately, these days, I have been unable to write to you as I had family problems.

I am sorry, dear diary, that the whole book is done. This is my last wish for you, as we have found a way to transport this hamster back to the sea, and I thank you a lot for your support in listening and understanding me in the darkest time.

Thank you, and bye.

H.Yashnashree

Story 30:
THE AVENGE OF DEATH

The waves uproared and splashed at his feet. The sand merrily wiped at his feet. The gale blew high, sending a rush of happiness onto the boy's head, sending his blonde, trusty hair fly strands of hair backward. The sand, which was greyish, mixed with the water and formed salty waves that fell on the boy's blue checked shirt. His rosy-like timber lips showed the agony of being alone. He could not go into the seaside house that was presented in chalky white with wet bricks and patches of paint falling. He made up his mind that he was not going in. The people who owned this place had hidden him from the world. Nobody knew that they were laboring kids like him in that place. He knew it was wrong to be labored. As a kid, he was taken into consideration as a servant. He had a pang of jealousy for the adults, who had their own petty lives while they worked for them. He immediately knew his name. He remembered that he had a nickname, Aarick. It meant being a lone ruler or a lone Viking. He was even as strong as a Viking, let alone his name. Soon, his nickname became his actual name.

He was as tired as a dark cloud, unable to hold his tears, which were rain. After one last gale, there came the rain splattering down his face. Feeling drowsy, Aarick squeezed his wadded - up shirt full of water and tramped into the back door. He had to find his way into the servant's cabin. He didn't want to bump into his master or mistress, for they whipped him with a fan or hard cane. He was unlike a horse wanting to be whipped to make him move. He was thankful that their master had not bought a flexible whip that was sharp enough to make anyone bleed. He had a few friends who were kind to him from the start. He was not so sure how he could get in without their master or mistress seeing him. He had the calibre to cheat them. Hoodwinking them made him happier at thought. In the backyard, there was his friend, Perrywinkle. She was 13 years old. She was an expert in gardening and was a gardener for their courtyards. Perrywinkle's brown hair was drenched in the rain, and he was merrily smiling, putting seeds in the soil. Aarick was 10 years old and was himself the butler for his master and mistress. Being a butler, he was not treated as harshly as the others'. He was the main servant out of everyone. Perrywinkle gazed at Aarick and whispered, "Hey Butler Aarick, I see something is coming into your mind." Aarick gave a mischievous twinkle in his eyes. Aarick whistled back, "Tell me when you have finished sowing." Perrywinkle gleamed at him," I have already wrapped up my work. Let's go according to your beat". Perrywinkle had a trolley of seeds and beckoned Aarick to jump inside it. Aarick smiled at her and jumped inside, covered in chucks of seeds. He had not been seen.

When she pushed the trolley and came to a halt in front of the servant's cabin, he emerged and pushed himself inside the door. There was a huge gossip in the servant's cabin, and everyone was excited to tell Aarick, something interesting. The carriage master was a young boy who was 9 years old named Christoper. He said that the master and mistress were pleased with your work. Tomorrow they are cutting a cake for your birthday and having a surprise field trip for you. We are all accompanying you as well. Aarick knew no bounds of happiness erupting within him. He was excited for the day ahead of him. He wondered what kind of cake it was going to be. He saw everyone having a twinge of jealousy towards him for being main and loved because he always did his work correctly without arguing with anyone. This made him special to the master and mistress. Aarick immediately washed his face, cleansed his arms, and wore his torn blue checked shirt with his purple pants. At once, he cuddled himself to his bed and was fast asleep on the rags before he knew it.

The next day, his master and mistress were excited for Aarick and had given him a bunch of new clothes. The clothes were very expensive, but they were from a thrift store. Aarick liked himself so much in the mirror that he wished to wear clothes like that every day. After blowing out his candles on the birthday cake, which was Belgian chocolate, he cut them into large pieces and gave them to the mistress and master. After giving it to them, he fed himself and his friends with the cake. Everyone loved the taste of it, and they all packed the picnic bag to go to the forest. All the kids were whipped by the mistress and master for packing the food. When the food was packed, the master and mistress cruelly pushed everyone and hit a few to start moving the carriage in which Aarick and their owner were sitting in the front seat. Aarick couldn't help but said to himself that he was a little cruel, and Aarick noticed that he, his mistress, and his master looked the same. When they reached the forest camp, all of them were very excited and started to unpack without heeding any advice. The master and mistress took him for a walk, and on their way there, they confessed that Aarick was actually their son, and they knew that everyone would blame him. They did not want him to suffer because of them. They abandoned him because they wanted a girl child and used him as a slave, but now the master and mistress were asking for mercy. Aarick yelled at them," What I heard now must be fake. I don't want to think of you as my parents. You are the cruelest parents in the world. I have done nothing to deserve slavery from you". He stormed off to join his friends to go to the circus. Meanwhile…. God had set foot on the regretful and guilty birthday of Aarick. God disguised himself as a girl in his twenties and had dropped a gift of unexpected joy. God knew the one thing that would make him happy, and he solemnly walked off. Aarick pounced on the circus tent. He first saw on the grass that laid a wrapped box. His curiosity knew no bounds and wanted to remove and see what was inside. He immediately tore open it, and there lay a gem of happiness. When he wore it, he did not know it was God's lesson for him.

In a thrice, the box sucked him into the world of happiness, where no labor was committed. The land was full of people smiling, and he became ecstatic and got around with everyone. He was friendly, and soon he smothered a smile. After a few hours, he wanted his normal life, as he realized that God can give happiness and sadness to those he loves. But when he was joyful, he started running to a porthole, which he found, and decided to go through it to go home. When he went, his leg slipped and his hands were grabbed, and half of it became stony and the rest was active and bouncy. Soon he slipped and fell unconscious, unable to retrieve himself again. Aarick felt himself leaving the world and begged God to catch him on his way. God did exactly what he wanted. Meanwhile, Aarick's wicked parents were unable to wash their sins away and were angrily searching the whole place. The kids, meanwhile, evacuated from the circus to help with the search. Nobody was too interested in the master and mistress' wishes. But, of course, they were worried about their butler friend. Everyone cried their hearts out, but for some reason, their mistress and master thought it was Christoper who had not been taken care of Aarick. They whipped him so hard on Christoper's neck that he left the world. Up aboard in heaven, there came Aarick, who was looking miserable and murmured to himself, "I just want to go back to my parents. I don't find God so good in heaven."

Aarick was accidentally transported to heaven as he was caught by God. Aarick would not help, but he was in a rage with God. He could not feel his heart burn at the sight of God, but he was miserably longing to go back to his parents, whom only he saw in his bad eyes and never felt so great in his good eyes. This time, he had met them with good eyes and wanted to be back with his parents. But his heart burned at the thought of being slaved by his parents. He could not believe the facts about his parents, nor neither him. He saved himself up to a hill where God was inviting new invitees to join in at heaven. In the queue, Aarick spotted someone facially familiar and went up to see him. But then he realized it was Christoper. "What is Christoper doing in heaven? Could he be searching for me?", Aarick thought. Christoper smiled and fell to God's knees. He looked up to see Aarick in front of God. "Aarick, you made me die because you hid over here, and you have got me killed by the master and mistress",Christoper yelled in despair. Aarick had a cruel motivation inside his heart and dare not let it out, and the moment Aarick got angry at Christoper, he snapped his teeth and growled angrily. Aarick begged God to leave him home, but God sighed and left him home in despair. God had lost Aarick just for the sake of happiness but decided to watch his next move. As soon as God lowered Aarick into the forest, he watched Aarick's next move. Aarick noticed the circus was over and the carriage where it had been parked had been taken away, and he was confused. As soon as Aarick did not know what to do, God squeezed through the clouds and held him gently and smiled," I knew you could not go further than you have. You can be here with me, but first wash away your own sins before committing a crime against them. I know you very well and no longer that your parents need you at home. As far as I know, they will be punished in a short time. You may now go and meet Christoper, whom you have been talking to as a friend. Now ask me a boon I may grant you unless it is not about your parents". "God, I have mistaken that you cannot read my mind. But, of course, you have been knowing that in my mind I wish I was as cruel as my parents. I promise you this sin will not be committed. Please, will you wash away my sins and teach me the Bible scroll? All the rhythms must be in my heart except for the cruelness, which should be squeezed away", Aarick responded. "My dear child, your sins are reversible, as you have regretted them, how about your parents?" God voiced out. Aarick and God gazed at each other gravely, but they knew that his parents' next life were not as great and cruel as their past life. "They will soon learn their lesson, as their incredible son has",God pointed out to Aarick. Somehow, his parents could not find him anywhere and were convinced that he had been killed by some wild animals. To sort it out, they tried to find him. They regretted the part where their son was a slave for them. They could not last their long life and knew that they

The Treasure Trove of Stories and Poems

were going to die, and of course they died very soon in the hope of having their son again.

Story 31:
Friendship leads to mishaps at times

Hails of snow glittered down the pavement. There were seas of hoodies and jackets. Juliana's cheeks were pink because of the cold, and her fingers became a little bonny and frozen stiff. Juliana shivered through her unmistakable black jacket, cuddling herself into it. Juliana was a lonely girl at 10 and was trying to make her way to 11 without the higher grades bullying her. It was hard for her to feel herself growing up because of the bullying that made her feel low. She wished that she was not a shy girl who would always be mute to others. She only had one best friend. It was her last day of school for the Christmas holidays before the next year's term initiated.

Her stray blonde hair was tied back with a ribbon, and she felt like feeling the warm air of sunshine that blew her hair now and then. It was so cold and windy for the weather to start a breeze. Juliana was heaving herself up the hill because she wanted to ice skate on the frozen lake nearby. Her parents had a set of activities in line for her. She was neither good at any of the activities like caroling, skiing, snowball fighting, baking cookies, nor dancing to the holly hymns. Her best friend also loved to ice skate as well. Her name was Melody. Melody was not to be seen anywhere around the ring. Juliana's blood pumped a high rise of sadness and betrayal. Where could her best friend have gone?

At once, she spotted a brunette girl who smiled prettily at everyone within her wavy hair. Juliana had a wave of relief rush over her as she bound off to meet her. At first, Melody did not reach Juliana's eye and was chattering away, but when Juliana silently tucked her arm from behind within Melody's arm, Melody pushed it away and brushed her arms away from the cold. Juliana did not know who the people were or why they were talking to her best friend?

All of them were kids of her age. Juliana couldn't help to think that Melody had got a new best friend and was no longer needed. Juliana felt she had mistaken the annoyed girl, thinking that she was the kind and loving Melody she knew. Instantly, at a glance, Juliana spied the girl's eyes, which were blue instead of green. She immediately ran off guard into the lake with her pair of ice skates, which she had strapped on, before she bounded off towards the girls.

Henceforth, Juliana muttered an awkward sorry as the girls who she had met up with accidentally all started laughing as she had tried to push in the conversation and also put in hands with a girl who Juliana had not known before.

Juliana skated far away from them as her cheeks became hot when she glanced backwards with shame. Her cheeks kept on burning hot as the shame in her body couldn't leave her alone. She was sad that Melody had not come and burned furiously.

With embarrassment, after one last round around the ring, she packed up her skate and strapped her fluffy boots and ran away before anyone could comment anything on her.

Juliana was just in time for caroling which was going to be proceeded at the square hall, where all the carolers of any age were presented to start singing. It was also appreciated by the mayors and the president to put in the kids who were good at singing. Their voices were as sweet as nectar, and they would learn all the songs immediately without any regrets.

The mayor was pleasantly proud of it and thought that was the greatest part of England as well. But thankfully, Juliana was not disconsolate anymore. She was thrilled, and to say the truth, even Melody was in the choir because of her sweet words, which were sung and weaved through sounds.

Everyone was also enlivened to see the choir. The crowd jumped up and down, waiting for the choir to appear. The choir, in a thrice, took its place with the head of an old lady who minded it," Let us start with today's biggest and most unstoppable choir. This will be amazing and interesting to every one of you present here. Have you had any kind of reason for this sweet, melodious rampage tonight? Are you all ready to hear this carol on Christmas Eve? I dearly thank Melody for her wonderful creativity on a new carol, and she says all thanks to her best friend for the support. Let us begin."

The carol....

"The will of love and heart to feel is sent by you.

Oh lord! We cannot dream of a day without you, so we sing the carol for you to bless us.

We are thankful for the deeds that you have done.

And we are delighted that you are here to help us.

We are grateful that you were born and that thy gave us life.

We won't cross the boundaries of who we are.

And will always remain the same.

We will always try to keep our love within us for you, and we will resource the natural uses that have been born from you as well."

Everyone gasped in happiness. Melody spotted Juliana and came rushing down in her long white gown. They both jumped at each other and hugged. They felt awful that they couldn't meet before the carol. Everyone happily rushed home in the evening light as Melody and Juliana tucked their hands together and skipped along the lane to a bakery that sells yummy gingerbread houses during Christmas. They got a warm feeling from buying it and feasting on it together. They planned a feast for Christmas dinner. The feast included: hot chocolate, cookies, a gingerbread house, buche de noel, fruit cake, mashed potatoes, eggnog, pudding with cranberry sauce, turkey, candy canes, ham, cake and mince pie. The best friends marched towards the building (the shop) to buy the food. They were outside the shop. When they saw an eerie glow in the shop, it had cobwebs and was full of darkness on the outside.

There was neither a holly nor a banner representing Christmas. There were no customers, but someone was flashing a torch in the shop. The girls immediately found it hard to believe that someone was there inside. They knew that no one could go inside unless the owner, Mr. Jacob, was available. He was poverty-stricken but dedicated to being a baker and finally became a famous baker. Everyone was looking at the two girls hesitantly. The girls were gaping at the shop.

A young teenager went up to the poor, heartbroken girls who were planning for the feast. The teenager whispered in their eyes," We all know you guys well, as Mr. Jacob has said that you are his regular customers. I am happy for you, but I have some unsettling news. Mr. Jacob had to go live with his aunt on the other side of town and could not take care of the shop. It remains shut. Hopefully, in his willpower, he will come back and stay."

Meanwhile, the man who hated working so hard, mostly during Christmas, loved to visit Mr. Jacob's shop, mostly as he loved the taste of each of the food items. Now that Mr. Jacob was away, he could not resist the smell, so he planned to steal as much as possible from the shop so that he could stuff his stuff and his family members. He stole six sacs of grubs. He was planning to steal it each day. It could have been fun to steal one grub per day. He thought of making his own pantry without others' knowledge so that he could complete the pantry and find out many of his hidden secrets, which he never revealed to anyone. He had stolen in through the back door, where his bodyguards were waiting for him. While he was busy flashing his light, he did not know that the girls had spotted the flashlight and had suspicious above suspicions.

The girls muttered between themselves and then thanked the

teenager. Juliana at once asked," Why did Mr. Jacob's aunt call him?" The teenager smiled at them and replied," The aunt was very old and unable to walk exactly that's why Mr.Jacob is not here."

Everyone breathed in silence at the likely explanation given by the teenager, and the teenager walked off, leaving the girls alone. The girls, meanwhile, planned to do some invading inside the shop to find out who was there. The question on who was there was not going to be likely explained unless someone took care of the problem that happened there.

Both the girls tried to find a way through the shop to get inside, but were likely so in need that they decided to go through the back door. But they noticed that it was occupied by two muscular bodyguards who were standing by the door and looking inside the door of the shop. There came a fat clerk wearing a tied waist suit who was brushing back his silky blonde hair. Anyone could say who he was. He was the mayor, Philari Jones, who had just been at the carols. What was he doing here? Was he stealing the money or food from the shop? The mayor had the grubs in his hand and was about to pass where the girls were hiding, but they appropriately jumped up from behind and surprised the mayor. The mayor got exasperated at the girls and shrieked," Who are you?". Melody yelled back at him, "My name is Melody, and she is my friend Juliana. We know that you are not stealing the money, but the grubs. But we have a warning for you. You can throw in all the grubs. If you choose to eat, then it is your fate."

The mayor said, "My family members and I just love eating his grubs, so I am taking all the grubs as this shop is out of stock. I will steal it." The girls spread the news about the mayor stealing the grubs. Soon, he was thrown away from the mayor position.

The poor mayor and the girls chuckled at the thought. The girls hated the thought of politics about electing the mayor, but the people had to give their names for the election as well. They sighed. It was a narrow escape that the mayor had left the girls free. The girls were super happy about it.

After a few days, the mayor decided to change and went to the election, begging them for a last chance and apologizing to them. Finally, the political people allowed him to become mayor. The girls finally noticed that Mr. Jacob had come back from town after some days.

Again, the girls were thinking about the same thing and went to the shop. They got the shock of their lives. They hadn't realized that the mayor had taken all the grubs needed. Mr. Jacob was informed about it by the girls and poor Mr. Jacob had to do twice the hard work and the girls accepted to help him do the goodies for Christmas. While Mr. Jacob was baking, the billionaire mayor shamefully bowed his head as he walked inside. He said, "Mr. Jacob, I beg your pardon for the greediness I had on your grubs, but now I like to do something in honor for you". He slowly took down a trophy from behind where he was hiding it and handed it over to Jacob. It was a Golden Jubilee award in baking. Suddenly, the mayor started laughing as he put it on the counter. He smelled the fresh cookies baking and said, "You can give this award for sale, and I am extremely delighted to give it to you." He sliced the back of the golden jubilee award and said," There is chocolate in this award and the secret plans for your upcoming fortunes, and I have given the recipes as well." Tears of happiness gleamed in Mr. Jacob's eyes as he thanked profusely to the mayor and as the mayor walked out, they both glanced at each other. Mr.Jacob made twice the money he needed that year. Then the girls bought the goodies from Jacob and happily went home. The girls celebrated their victory by having a feast. They also hung their holly on the garden gate.

H.Yashnashree

Story 32:
Christmas story

The aroma of freshness bathed the glaciers, and through the dust of cobwebs, a dingy old bakery stood. Nobody in London dared to go inside, and during the frosty weather, there were smells and silent voices inside the bakery. The bakery was usually dark, but during the holidays, on Christmas, it was lit up, and curious sounds were to be noticed. This is where I live. I am Annabelle, the elf, and my family and thousands of elves live here with me. We love making garments and toys for Santa to deliver them out to kids. Santa always works hard on delivering the gifts while we make the toys. My parents were toymakers, as they had been given the role to do that. Other elves had to stitch dresses, make food, or take care of the magical reindeers. The joy of happiness lifted up the spirits of enjoyment and love. I had always wanted to become a chef captain in our Elves community. Maple syrup and fruits were stirred in pots. Other flavors were added. When they finally took it out, the result was fruit cake. The fruit cakes were platted among the dishes for all of us. We were all seated from work to have a great deal of fruit cake. But then, at once, Platza immediately found herself through this joyous occasion. I instantly wondered if her greeting card for her parents was missing or that the hollies, which we stitched so hard, were torn apart by mice. I, being a star chef, immediately predicted that something of our food were gone missing, and I was right.

The maple syrup, berries and fruit cakes were all finished, and we elves, famished by hard work, had eaten it all away. Meanwhile, nobody was interested in that problem. They started rounding me up, and when they cornered me, they told me once for all that I should become an astrologer, and that would make us all proud. When I tried to reassure them, it was just a guess, and nobody believed me. Not even my parents were interested in hearing my protest, so I needless to say that I had to give an excuse to them by saying,"Me and Platza could go out for maple syrup and fruits?" "Yes," everyone agreed to it. After everyone agreed with what I had told them, I immediately took Platza's hand and whispered in her ear," Do you believe me or not?". She replied, "Yes". We both held hands and decided to go to the market and buy some provisions.

Immediately, I got a clever idea. That idea danced to and fro in my mind, and a mischievous gleam encountered me. I hurriedly took three precious things from my family, my father's magical sewing needle, my mother's glasses (wonky glasses) and a tapestry book filled with legends of elves. I pocketed them safely. I and Platza went out of the door silently to the market. I told Platza about my plan and before we knew it, there was an utmost rush to the market. When we came back home rejected, all of them were impatiently waiting for me. When I entered the door, all of them had five gifts each for me for the celebration of Christmas. I opened it, there was normal stuff, and most of it was astrology books. There were elves, philosophers and teachers telling me the facts of the astrology of the moon and sun. There were gold passes to the astrology school, and my mom was proud of me and was showing off about me. Everyone was clearly begging me after the gold pass. Now, it was time to put the plan into action. I neatly put the stuff in a different container. My parents now badly needed it, so I used my fake prediction and told them where it was. They were now super proud, as I got things out of prediction. Meanwhile, I told them how glad I was to help them and Platza merrily told my parents that whilst I and Annabelle were in the market, we found a school on astrology and it would take 5 years to graduate and Annabelle was supposed to go there as her name was qualified on the list. Hearing this, my parents were swelled up with pride and made Platza and me go together to fake astrology school. Meanwhile, Platza and I were sent packing off the road towards the school. But then we reached a far distance and burst out laughing. There was a car waiting for us to drive me off to culinary school, and I finally reached the top of my ambition. Platza, who was happy for me, wished me a merry Christmas and gave me a huge basket filled with candies.

As I waved goodbye, I noticed the roads filled with snowmen looking up above the sky as the stars were twinkling so bright. As usual, Platza went out of humming to their elf colony with triumph in her eyes.

The Treasure Trove of Stories and Poems

H.Yashnashree

Story 33:
The Colosseum (ESSAY)

From the bloody battles to the corpses and through the secret tunnels, I bring you the realistic journey of the Colosseum. This building is with limestone and stones and its magnificent arches proudly show the features of it being one of the seven wonders of the ancient period. It tells us the lives slain due to the aggressiveness of entertainment for the citizens and emperors of Rome. The Colosseum holds the title of the biggest amphitheater in the world. The amphitheater is known for its 100 games entertained by the citizens and the emperor. The emperor, who is known for being bathed in his cruelness and his mounting wealth for which everyone cursed, was Emperor Nero. Emperor Nero witnessed that he was running out of money and that was when he knew he had given it all for his luxurious villa, which he named 'The Golden Palace'. When he died, the successive four emperors who came into the palace also died. Emperor Vespasian was immersed in the beauty of Rome and the benefits of clothing, cultural activities and amphitheatres. When he learned there was no Emperor, he seized the throne for the greatest power of expanding Rome. Seeing that Emperor Vespasian only cared about his citizens and their health, they began to show dedication and obedience to him. Emperor Vespasian noticed that Rome did not have any landmarks and entertainment, he established the plan of the amphitheatre, the Colosseum. Under his supervision, the lake of the Golden Palace, which was in honour of Nero, was drained and taken down in force. Linking through the ground the abysses of secret passages led to different dungeons.

The secret passages were to hide the gladiators and animals in training for the next combats. From 70 to 72 BC, he struggled with illness after the construction and his son Titus was to rule. Emperor Titus also died after the construction of the Colosseum. Domitian, the newly crowned emperor, completed the Colosseum and opened it for the honourable games to start. Each structure and part is made to be marveled and each layer has a coat made to be vigorous as well, brought up to the movement of victory and loss over life and death. Limestone heated with a putty mixture and powdered concrete shapes itself into the beauty and pride of the Colosseum. The rocky and uneven texture of the bricks and concrete was hardened to the touch, and the touch fills our hearts with sadness as the beauty and importance of the Colosseum are far away to be felt. Dozens of slaves sitting on the gravel path waited for the moment for the freedom and liberation of their work. They were overjoyed to hear that the construction of the Colosseum would require many slaves. Specifically, the beaten and unforgivable slaves were working as hard as ants. The approximate number of slaves who worked for the construction of the Colosseum was 60,000 to 100,000. The slaves who wanted to attain freedom and liberation were startled to hear that they had to build a road near the town of Albulae, which in the present is known as the Town of Tivoli. 240,000 wheelbarrows were pushed by the road for more bricks to build the Colosseum. The bricks that were held in the wheelbarrow were 3250 stones.

The bricks were loaded on the Colosseum for the structure to begin and take shape and to understand the meaning of life in the Roman Empire. Once this structure was constructed, everybody was excited to come to the Roman amphitheatre. In the excitement and anticipation, they soon got seated and were ready to see the games. The games were the most exciting and unusual for everyone. Parades were sent down in the amphitheater, then there were executions of religious people with sacrifices, and animals were hunted, followed by gladiator fights, horse races and novakia battles(ship mock battles). The seats that hung up and down to show the entertainment were classified by status and value. The front seats right next to the arena were the people of royalty and other rich merchants and families who were seated to be entertained. The second and third rows were for generals and men. The last row, which was in the higher nook facing like a hawk, neither could hear nor see. This was the place given to the women and the slaves and on the summer days they were the luckiest, as there was an awning that was meant as a ship canvas sail that was plastered onto the sides of the Colosseum to shelter people from sunstroke. There are many great poets as well, viewing the prospects of the Colosseum's enchanting entertainment through the front row. There was the poet Maximus, who was vulnerably great at making horror turn into goodness. There was a saying that the poet Valerius Maximus had written a poem about something horrible that had happened in the Colosseum. He says that a man named Rufus was screwed to fear in a dream in which a gladiator had killed him in the Colosseum during the battle. The next day, Rufus was accompanied by his friends to the Colosseum and sat in the front row. Rufus felt that it was his last and was nearing his death, and he could do nothing to stop it from happening.

As the gladiator combats had started, he recognized the gladiator from his dream and persuaded his friends to let him go to his home, but was sadly joked at to his sorrow and was dragged to watch the games. Rufus then watched the gladiator kill his opponent, and to give him one last blow, the sphere was accidentally rushed into the air and hit Rufus in the heart and of course, he died. There was also a myth of a giant Indian python who had escaped the Colosseum's arena and was rumored to have killed children in the slum. There was an attack in which a rogue leopard jumped on an artist and Domitian, the emperor, complained on rigging the games so that his favorite gladiator always won. That spectator was thrown in the arena to be fed by the wild dogs. The Romans never felt bored, as they had available toilets, food stalls and wine sellers. They also had ball-breaking cash prizes to go to their spot on an island, which was known as a normal apartment. It would be a great honor to be an empress of imagination. I would like to stop gladiator hunts if possible for non-harmful entertaining games.

Story 34:
The scarab of chambers

I breathed, whimpering softly. The tomb of Cleopatra creaked open. My heart raced. There was a scarlet light beaming from the tomb. The treasures of the tomb seemed to bow low. I, Yashnashree, an author and topper of the class, was not creating it up.

There was my ticket for researching Cleopatra and other pharaohs. Before I knew it, I had played and was with my friends at the museum. As I was telling you, when I reached the area of Cleopatra's tomb with my friends, it had started to open with the scarlet light beaming upon us. Everyone froze and began to feel scared. Treasures glinted in the light while bowing. The place was so silent that I broke it, "What is happening?"

Suddenly, a cyclone swirled over the museum. The tomb started to suck up stuff around it before I had time to move. My best friend who tried to pull me back, were sucked together inside the tomb. Me being the first favorite student of my favorite teacher, she couldn't bear to see me vanish away, so she came in as well.

Meanwhile, I noticed that another lump of a person was following us down the spiral hole. When I finally got to see her face, it was my favorite teacher. When we three landed, we noticed a long hissing sound coming from the corridor above us. We had somehow fallen into a chamber where no one knew how to get out. As a result, I realized that we were in the hidden chamber of Cleopatra, where she had died last.

There were traces of blood vanishing and rising as puddles. There was a set of salt water poured on the ground and a huge knife splattered with blood around the edges. There were historical pictures painted and carved around the vast area. The whole chamber was empty when the familiar hissing noise started again. My teacher, Prema Mam, worriedly said," It feels like being in a dream". My best friend Srismruthi, worriedly nodded her head, casting a glance at me.

Meanwhile, I was busy trying to find out if something matched up here with the research that I had done. I started drumming my hands on the wall while saying to myself," Find the scarab, the beetle god who raises the sun, or the dot with a circle around it representing the sun."

Once I had finally found the beetle, I pressed on it. I was wondering if there was an exit passage through the graffiti, but I had gotten a shock that could never leave me at all. There was a secret cabinet, and in that, I could see the unmistakable crown poking in and there, reading out as a scroll in a string of Egyptian words that I could understand.

I saw black hair twirling around the shelves, and right then I saw her eyes, the ones lined with Egyptian kohl, blue and full of mystery. She saw me and walked with full dignity as I strutted backward. When I saw her face-to-face, I screamed out, "Cleopatra." My best friend and teacher froze immediately and were looking like they were about to faint. I instantly noticed another scarab along the corridor. I was debating with myself whether I could go and touch the scarab or run away, dragging my friends to the topmost floor in the hidden chamber.

So, I ghastly thought in a flash of brainstorming that was going on in my mind. I immediately buckled out my beet and tied it around the waists of my teacher's and friend's. I then removed the extra belt of Srismruthi's and tied it around me. When Cleopatra noticed it, she started brandishing a sword that was draped on her thighs. When she had pulled it out, the blood in it was dripping wildly enough, and I started racing my speed as Mam jogged with my friend for their lives.

I noticed that we were almost reaching the scarab, and Cleopatra was unable to keep up with us as we reached the scarab. She roared Egyptian victory cries as she came after us. I at once pushed the scarab into the brick, and there was another opening, which was a room filled with paintings and manuscripts, and there was a person near the mirror who I could not recognize. When Cleopatra noticed him, she immediately went running and wrapped her arms around him.

In a thrice, I identified him as well. I quickly signaled to my friend and mam to follow me up silently as we pushed ourselves and walked amongst the shadows. I once again saw another scarab. I realized that there were many hidden rooms and cabinets because of the sun and scarabs.

As I reached the third room and pushed open the scarab for the hidden room, it left me speechless. There was the always friendly Gaius Julius Caesar. As soon as he noticed us, he smiled at us, welcoming us to his study room.

When we entered his study, we were for sure breath-taken by the astounding library and manuscripts. He was reading a fragile paper in the library but when he heard Cleopatra screaming for Julius Caesar and telling him about the prisoner wandering around the area, finding hidden doors. We were shocked, and I almost felt ill being incredible by seeing the history that had journeyed into the present.

My teacher fell back and panted. I reached out my hand and urged her forward. As I did so, the belt fell down, and I slipped down the steps. I could feel the faces above me as the world faded behind me. I could hear buckets of water been thrown at my hair. It smelt like dust or garbage Red-colored lines were circling before me and I immediately assumed that I was in for an execution where no one could save me.

I heard the sound of wailing and also heard Miniac laughing. Those laughs were ringing in my ear, and I was ever doubtful that something awful was happening. I could detect a whoosh of hair coming like a rocket above my face. My hands were interweaved so tightly that the rope, which seemed to be compacted, could barely move an inch.

When I opened my eyes, there were chains around my legs and I was being dragged away silently. I was about to protest when I saw my teacher quietly hovering me out of the room inaudibly. Whilst, she did that, Srismruthi was slowly using her Swiss army knife to cut the rope to set me free. As I was out, I beheld a cosmic pot in which Cleopatra's talent for making portions was flaunted in limestone to show her real identity as a witch.

There were dead animals and meat pressed against each wall. Portions and plants were in cut form as roots and other parts were poisoned, and toxic flowers adorned a massive compartment on the shelf. I thought I had seen a skull as well. I then realized that we were in Cleopatra's lab.

Everyone in the room was dead silent and had minded their own business. The doorway was the mouth of Pharoah, and the wooden door seemed to be slightly opened. When we disassembled, I breathed a sigh of relief, and I protested what had happened when I had fainted.

My teacher first led us feebly to the chamber's loft, where she compressed the scarab, invoking another hidden room. Unlike the other rooms, this seemed to carry the most precious of precious secrets ever seen in the world. There was a small cot in which there was blood splattered all over it. I quietly commented," This must be the area where Cleopatra died in the legendary heroic act of killing herself by an asp in a noble gesture. This noble gesture not only ended her life but was also because of the killing assassinations of Mark Antony and Cleopatra.

We three cleared a spot in the cot of blood. We were not only petrified but also wondering what had happened so terrible that it had hurt her feelings. It was a little troublesome to think of it as the doom of the queen. I immediately noticed a flap in the corner of the room.

My teacher explained," Yashna, when you fainted, me and Srismruthi rushed to you, but Cleopatra was quicker than us. She and Julius Caesar dragged you by the leg and tied you to the rope, then Cleopatra summoned Mark Antony to guard her secret portion lab while she tried to feed you a wretched portion. By the time Julius Caesar tripped over, from running and catching us. So we saw another scarab and we came here to hide. Julius Caesar and Mark Antony had not seen where we had gone. So, they started chattering and went to sit near the door. Slowly, they descended the chamber and when they did that, me and Srismruthi immediately and quietly stepped into the lab and dragged you as fast as we could out of the door, and we did succeed.".

Meanwhile, I had noticed a huge sable shadow loomed over us and I enormously feared that it was Cleopatra. She had a sword in her hand, and I closed my eyes in desperation not to leave this world. I decided to think fast. I grabbed my teacher's and friend's hands and rushed forward to the flap in the room. What surprised me the most was that there was enough room to pull in 10,000 people, and when I went in, there were baskets that were large enough to fit three people into it.

I wondered what was going to happen, but I wasn't going to wait. I hopped into the front seat while my teacher and friend hopped into the back. We loaded ourselves, and when my weight pushed, the basket itself moved tremendously through a huge track line. When we started flying through everything, we realized that the ghost was not approaching anymore and we were going to the present by this weird basket.

I at once ascertained that this was not an actual ghost that was appearing by a vampire's heed or an amulet, but it was a ghost of the cat goddess (Bastet). I immediately understood that the starting life of the cat in ancient Egypt was when a kitten would be born and lay on the carrier basket to be taken to their new home, then jumped out of the basket and be flanged down. I told my teacher and friend to follow me, but at first they thought I had gone a little cuckoo. Reluctantly, they hurled down after me.

I yelled,"Do you know anything we can do to prevent ourselves from falling and hitting the ground". Finally, we noticed the transformation in the basket rather than being a normal basket, it had turned into a cat goddess (Bastet), and behind her henceforth, there was Cleopatra and her men. I silently nodded to my teacher, telling her that this was the reason.

My teacher suggested," Why can't you use a rope or a plastic cover?" I silently said," Plastic is not invented in this era." She muttered," Does that mean we are going to die of starvation and being bruised by falling down?". Now each of us was reaching the ground, and there was nothing to do. We were helpless, and at once, there was a flash indicating our fall, dashing to the ground. We were getting fearful, but then the floor opened, and we were sitting in our school bus, going back home. When we were on the bus, I mischievously smiled and forced myself to show four scrolls that I had stolen from the area to be distributed to the museum and to know the real life of Cleopatra.

The Treasure Trove of Stories and Poems

Story 35:
The Revolutionary Change

Chapter 1 : The Parchment Leads to misery

The dark, silvery sky twinkled with bright stars and shimmered with a sleepy and wistful light from the moon. Glinting through the stars, a shooting star fell upon the village in a dazzling gleam, showering upon every inch of the world. The mist fogged, and the water sent a cold breeze upon the surrounding land. At the top of the eagle's eye, on the northern cliff, dwelled a fortune teller and her granddaughter. One word to describe them was serene. The granddaughter was beautiful in her looks, talents, and wisdom. Ariel, with her flowing blonde hair and her grandmother Bethany, wondered if there was more she wanted to discover in her life or if she was fine being cooped up in her house.

Her grandmother was chubby, with white hair and black spectacles. She was a sort of grandmother who was into cooking, magic tricks, fortune balls, and story-telling. That night, her grandmother, 69 years old, was busy cleaning a dusty fortune ball when she stumbled upon a map. Ariel, who was dimly lighting up a lamp, noticed her grandmother holding up a piece of parchment, and she trotted towards her grandmother's side with an air of mystery.

The lights were on around the house, and the dark forest adjoining the house lit up as well. "Ariel!", her grandmother echoed," What do you think you are doing in the middle of the night?" Ariel susurrated moodily as she circled the shape of the fortune ball, telling anxiously," I smelt something in our wardrobe and was about to open it. When I heard the sound of the rustling of paper and dust, I decided to wake up". Her grandmother smeared ink blots over the parchment as she wrote a sentence and started to cry, wobbling widely. She snatched a huge psychology book and began to read while drying her eyes. She muttered under her breath in dolor relief.

Ariel heard it and immediately thought that something with the wrong conclusion was written on that parchment. She, being 13 years old, had memorized all the words in the dictionary and told herself," Books are a pain reliever for grandma, and what made her cry so loudly is my suspicion. I must look into that letter before my grandma knows it".

Ariel absent-mindedly took a feather from the top of the book shelf and inaudibly placed it in her hand. She cupped her hand and draughted the feather in it. The feather kinked its way to her feet. The feather was cosmetic and delicate. It was the softest feather that anyone had ever seen. It was pure orange, as she had held it with curiosity exploding in her heart. When her grandma took it from the floor, it turned blue(wisdom).

Her grandma slowly mouthed Ariel to go back to bed. Ariel unhappily dissipated with the click of her heels. She decided that it was too late to go back to bed as it was 5 o'clock early in the morning, but her mind doubted that it couldn't be. She swarmed her eyes towards the shadowy, creepy vintage grandfather clock in the hall. She hid her disappointment by biting her lips. It was still 1' o'clock; she called her grandma, asking her the exact time. Her grandma yelled back at her," It is 5 o'clock." Ariel morosely grabbed a pair of gloves and a set of tools and started to repair the grandfather clock.

Whilst, Ariel was doing that, her grandma told her to mind the house as she went to buy a pail of milk from the nearby provision store. Ariel's eyes gleamed with determination as she noticed her grandma was going out. She jumped up out of happiness, as this was the ticket to the mystery. Ariel washed her hands, waltzed through the hall and came to stop at the entrance of the hall. What she saw was completely horrifying.

Chapter 2:Desires with a Pail of Milk

"Bethany! Today you woke up so early!", joked Mia, the shopkeeper of the provision store. "Mia, Do you know anything that is left under your allegiance from my ancestors?", Bethany questioned. Mia fearfully nodded and gave her a huge pail of milk, which Bethany had asked for.

Bethany hurried home just in time to see everything uncluttered. The grandfather clock ticked by and the shelves were neatly arranged. Her granddaughter did not know where she had hidden it, but when she reached out to her book on psychology and opened the first two pages, to her trepidation, she noticed the binder being tagged out in a dire manner, ripping out the sheets with the plastic cover.

What Bethany had experienced was a yellowish, faded parchment. She pondered that it could be Ariel who had taken it.

Chapter 3:Cookie on the Prowl

Apple cores were splattered everywhere. Portions were stacked upon each other all over the place. Creepers grew inside and tangled the veins of it and wrapped itself around, ropes were plaited into the ladders. There was a high chamber above, there were endless corridors, and each of it was lit by a candle. The candle wax dripped from each side and there was cardboard lying here and there. Pools of water dripped around, and peels of fruits were disposed of in every nook and cranny of the area.

Dust and cobwebs gathered around, with a skeleton's head lying around the domicile. It was a hidden area not known to anyone except for a resident known as the Cookie Monster. He could shape-shift into anything, and he had won the trust of the King of Candy Land, for his shape was always a cookie monster. He was always helpful to the people over there and did not neglect his duties of visiting the king and speaking about business stocks.

The king, who made the arrangements for him to stay there, was pleased that he didn't decline the offer. The cookie monster was being rewarded for his kindness and his respectable honesty, mostly with the princess, but he was not honest at all times. He was extremely pleased that no one had seen him dig a hole in the chocolate mud and take a route underground, which directed him back to his real house.

The mud that was splattered around his body gave him an idea of his appearance. He transformed himself into a delicious mud chocolate cookie. He knew that he had a bad influence on getting much more money to become wealthy.

He never felt bad about not working hard for money but only felt encouraged and full of elation. His mind diverted to a woman holding a fortune ball, and next to it was the parchment that he had been seeking for years.

Chapter 4: Glinting to where your heart desires

Ariel sadly rummaged through the shelves, trying to identify the parchment. When she didn't find it, she had noticed the book on psychology and opened the first two pages. She felt horrified when she noticed that the parchment was taken out with such force that it left no trace. She then saw a huge lump wrapped in a cover (package) that had gathered around dust and the letters written there gave her mind a complete diversion. She tore open the lumpy package, peering in woefully. An air of curiosity surrounded her as she pulled the mystery out from inside. She touched the delicate, soft material and stroked it under her fingers. She gently tugged at it, revealing a shiny golden carpet with silver lacings. It was studded with rubies, sapphires and emeralds that were pierced among the border, plus there was huge cushioning in the middle.

Ariel sighed optimistically, "This would make a great rug for my room". She then realized it was her grandma's and that she had no choice but to keep it back where it was. Ariel then wanted to once brush out the dust and sat on it, feeling full of her desires. After her hard work of cleaning the house, she laid down on the carpet, wriggling around. She finally stuffed it back where it was and left it on the ledge of the house.

Again, the same desire rose in her mind. Ariel reluctantly pulled out the carpet, and when she laid down on it, she took a cookie or two from her grandma's secret stash. The crumbs fell everywhere, throwing chocolate cream around herself and the carpet. Before she had time to lay her head relaxing on the carpet, it began wobbling. When she screamed, the carpet began moving and it rose higher and higher. Ariel screamed for help thus, she noticed a few letters that were sewn on the carpet.

She cleared out the dust and read it out, 'FLY WHERE YOUR HEART DESIRES'. Ariel remembered that when she was young, her grandmother had gone out walking and that was when she sneaked into her private study, where she found the recipes for sweets and healthy stuff. Her grandma usually never gave her candy or sweets, which made her have a tireless desire for them. Each recipe book's chapter on sweets was torn out.

Her heart desired first to go to Candy Land.

Chapter 5: The debate of wishes

Terror sang in her eyes, and her heart beat fast. Bethany knew that everything of hers was lost if there were no signs of the parchment. She noticed cookie crumbles stolen from her stash of cookies. Her magical carpet's package had been torn out, and there was not even a single trace of it to be found anywhere.

Her right window was broken, and the glass was shredded around the house, Bethany muttered to herself,"Why was I even in a hurry to transport the package of the magical flying carpet immediately using magic straight through the window?".Bethany had the power to transport things from one place to another using magic, but sometimes her magic was out of practice. Bethany searched for Ariel everywhere but was unable to find her. Dark clouds of gloom and doom circled across her eyes. She was unable to find her beloved granddaughter, and that meant she had gone on the flying magical carpet, but could she have stolen the parchment too? She tensely reached out to her dusty fortune ball. She had not witnessed that the fortune ball was vandalized and cracked all over the sides. It's smooth, round sides were molding themselves into an irregular shape. Bethany rubbed it twice and sang a wish:

Form me a grant
Which again I will never rank
Please do tell me about the past, which I see through you.
You bring me joy with your full hue.
To make me the one I can count on as special
Let me see who took the parchment.
And what did my granddaughter do when I was away?

The fortune ball lit up and showed only a few pictures. She saw an irregular shape taking her parchment away, and it looked nothing like Ariel. Bethany froze and swiped the fortune ball again. The next picture showed Ariel, with her full curiosity bounding over the magical carpet and her eyes full of glee.

Could Ariel have gone to Candy Land because she craved sweets all the time? She could have also gone to the haunted house, which she always wanted, but having no agreement in her mind, she debated aloud, "Ariel must have gone to the candy land, as it is her priority of all, for she has never tasted a sweet before in her life".

She crossed her fingers, hoping for good luck on her granddaughter's adventure in Candy Land. At the same time, she was curious about who had taken the parchment away. But on the other hand, she could not help but feel enraged at Ariel's behavior. "How could Ariel have lost refuge in her wisdom and, not controlling her curiosity, gone seeking something she never wanted? .That was highly impossible to think of", Bethany thought.

Chapter 6: The change of name

"My dear admirers, I would have never done this work without you",sounded Cookie Monster. "Cookie monster, you are a very good shape-shifter, so what should we call you?", asked one of the chefs in Candy Land, named Butler. The chef had been highly impressed by the cookie monster and had pursued a few of his best friends to meet his dear deity, the cookie monster. Lemon, Biscuit, Vanilla and Strawberry were the best friends of Chef Butler. They were too highly impressed by the cookie monster.

The shadow of the moon became darker as they called the cookie monster as Umbriel. The cookie monster slowly shifted his way into a huge dark shadow, wearing the black cloth over his whole body except his eyes."You may call me master at all time, if you dare to disrespect the great Umbriel, you must be thrown in the dungeons, and I will force you to give away your valuable things to me", announced Umbriel.

He ordered slowly Strawberry and Vanilla,"You both will go to Candy Land and see whether you have new visitors or not? If you do not find anyone, do not stop searching; go to other areas. If the visitor requires help, make them trust you and bring them here to me". Vanilla bowed down and requested, "Would you please shape-shift me into a horse to make myself more helpful to bring the visitor to you?".

"Yes, of course," Umbriel permitted.

Chapter 7: Guidance from the fake

Ariel's heart brimmed with joy as the glow reflected. As she hummed, she noticed two living beings made of candy roaming around in the woods. They were a little suspicious. She began to drop down from the carpet, and the carpet folded itself so tiny that there was no sign of it being seen. She noticed a beautiful candy horse leaning across a tree with its owner, Strawberry (Vanilla disguised as a horse).

Ariel rushed over to the troop and said,"I must find candy land, and I don't know how long it takes. Please guide me". Strawberry and the horse gaped at each other. They were happy that they had finally completed their quest. Strawberry said,"Alas! I am very tired of guiding this horse. He is going forth for execution, as he bit my master, so you can take this horse and pretend it's yours, and I will tell my master that this horse has been executed properly, so there is no use of me having him and taking guidance from him".

Ariel sat on it, and they began the journey. The horse slowly walked to Candy Land and showed her the grocery store nearby. Ariel did not realize how hungry she was until then! She ran into the gingerbread store and, on returning with a recipe book and a few packets of cheese and chocolates, she mounted back.

As they went into the heart of the city, they noticed a gate to the chocolate woodland. The grass was made up of sugar. Ariel munched on the cheese as she stared at it in awe. She pulled the reins of the horse inside and stopped at a clearing. She rested on the grass and hopped a few pieces of cheese immediately into her mouth. At once, four animals trotted out of nowhere. One was the bird, a reindeer, a rabbit, and an adorable yellow fluff standing right beside her. They patiently explained to her that they were the animals of guidance. The rabbit held up a candy cane and mentioned," We know that you are in danger and that horse is not a real one. We have been having an enemy of the candy land who has won the trust of our candy king. We are trying to give hints about the candy demolisher, but nobody believes us. His real name is Umbriel and nick nickname is Cookie Monster."

The bird pacified Ariel and said," We know what is written in that parchment, whatever you do, bring the parchment back to your grandma. My name is Flora. I was your grandma's pet when she was young. But I flew away from her and became one of the animals' guides in Candy Land. I will tell you what is written on the parchment. It is...

My dear,

You cannot lose hope because I am not there with you, but I will give you advice. Come to Candy Land and meet me, where there is a huge area. There, I will give you something more valuable. A four-clover lucky leaf that will make everyone love you. It will give you more than love—eternity and immortality. I hope you will be alright."

Ariel broke the silence and asked," Who wrote this note?". Flora replied cheekily," I did." Flora slowly admitted," I am such a magical creature that I can even write as well. That's how I wrote this bye-bye letter."

Soon after getting Ariel the lucky charm, Ariel pounced on the horse, looped a noose around the horse's neck, dragged it back to the forest clearing, shoved the horse aside, and said, "I want the parchment, and you are going to steal it from your master and hand it over to me". Slowly, Flora appeared and whispered something in Ariel's ear. Ariel gasped in shock," Oh no! This must be the reason why Umbriel took it".

Flora said in her ear that there was a secret area full of lucky charms, and the location was mentioned in the letter. The horse feared for his master and said," No, I have come on a mission to take you to my owner, but I have got an idea that will make both of us safe, after that, you are allowed to go."

Ariel nodded her head while the horse pondered the plan over and over again until Ariel understood. Ariel pretended to enjoy the ride on the horse while galloping to Umbriel. When they reached Umbriel's area, the gateway slowly creaked open. Umbriel smiled in as he welcomed them and said," Well, well, who do we have here today? Now, come here, Vanilla, I am going to give you another mission to solve. You will take $3/4^{th}$ of the treasure from my possession if you find me the lucky charm".

The horse pushed down Ariel as she sighed," I already know who you are, and if you are executing me, I am ready to be executed, but only by…"

Umbriel roared,"What is it, girl?. I am ready to execute you in every way. I know that I am the person who got your parchment, and to add to that, I have broken many pieces of furniture at your home and have also taken your spare fortune ball for myself, so now I know that you are coming. I decided to kidnap you and take all your possessions for me."

"Well, it was very kind of you to tell me that, but sadly, I can escape", Ariel mocked. She gratefully pulled out her folded magical carpet, swooped the parchment from Umbriel's hand, and circled through the gap of the gate before it was locked. She bayed,"Thanks for opening the gate".

Epilogue

Stars of happiness shimmered in her eyes as she reached her tucked-in cottage. She went in and saw her grandma, full of happy tears. Ariel immediately hugged her. Soon, grandma asked her," Why did you take my flying carpet?". Helplessly, Ariel shrugged," I wanted to go on an adventure to Candy Land, and so I went".

Meanwhile, at the rejoicing moment at the cottage, the fury and rage exploded among the people of Umbriel. Umbriel agitated and ordered the Butler," You must transform into a horse and wait for the same visitor. I do not care, even if it takes a year, but you must not come back".

Even till now, Butler has kept waiting for Ariel.

While in the cottage, Bethany, who had later received the lucky charm from Ariel, blew it out of the window and made sure that immortality was received by the person who fairly believed in it.

Bethany was anxious and told Ariel that, as the carpet was old, it took time to work. She didn't mind, but she felt that clarifying her granddaughter's queries was harder. She bought five recipe books on sweets for a revolutionary change and presented the carpet and parchment safely inside the shelf. Ariel was blessed with sweets because of her great feat.

Plan for stealing the parchment:

Cookie monster wins the trust of Butler, chef of the Candy Land.

Increases his population.

Makes butler to hide in Ariel's cupboard to steal the parchment (P.S smelly)

After sleeping, the parchment was stolen.

The sentence which was written by Bethany in the parchment was 'F A N – means February or April or November (for getting lucky charm)'.

The End

H.Yashnashree

Story 36: Monalisa

"If I were you, I would rather read a book", Evelyn curiously mumbled to her older sister Valentina. It was their summer holidays and there was nothing more enjoyable to Evelyn than reading. Valentina, getting disinterested in her younger sister, decided to spend time on her own. Valentina's friends were busy as it was the summer holidays. Meanwhile, she dug out some ideas and then she planned them. She decided to manipulate her sister into having a picnic by the riverside. She looked into their bedroom to find her sister, not realizing that she was not always the victim she could have been. So, she ventured out on her own, depicting no loneliness and thought she might have a big feat of her own. Evelyn actually had her own play time after completing her book. She opened a huge treatise from her shelf and whispered to it," I will take one leap and you should transport me anywhere". She shook the treatise and to her delight, her spirit animal began walking towards her. It was a lion, the Leo.

It warned her," You cannot let anybody see me and if they do, wherever you go, you will be embedded". Evelyn hurriedly nodded and locked the door. She whispered to herself, "Wherever you are taking me, let it be thrilling". She took her camera and encyclopedia and pocketed them safely. The treatise opened and with one roar, it went back to the shelf. Leo roared again and the mouth was massive, it immediately sucked her in. Evelyn looked for guidance as she was in its mouth. She saw a spinning portal next to her and she jumped into it. The next thing she knew was, that she was directly in front of the Eiffel Tower. She took out her camera and took a snap of it. Then she leaped towards it and as Leo promised, she was transported to the Louvre Museum. It was located on the bank of the Seine. She raced up to the muesum's entrance and walked inside. Her first step in looking at the art was the Monalisa. She immediately rushed towards it and shakily took a picture. Before deleting it, she once again took a picture, which was evident and accurate. It was perfect and she loved it. She again pocketed her camera, but before that, she knocked into the French technician named Pascal Cotte. He was working hard to find out the Monalisa mystery. Evelyn lost her senses as she was shy and when Pascal approached her, she squirmed a little, which led to swiping the camera's surface. The ugly picture that she had snapped before came to the screen and before she could do anything, Pascal asked her that where was her parents. She gave him a lame excuse and was about to run away when he caught sight of the ugly picture on the camera and asked her that if he could see it. Gladly handing over the camera, he addressed her, "Young lady, it is more surprising that you found a decoded message in this picture. Please come with me and tell your parents to accompany you if you need it." Evelyn said," It is not necessary". So, Pascal ordered his assistants to bring him the paintings of Monalisa from the Louvre and Isleworth Monalisa.

Having the camera in her hand, she did not realize that she was getting to fulfill her dreams of becoming a scientist. She looked into her camera, the photo looked like blurry dimensionality of two Monalisa's, but with their hands clasped as if in a sacred position. "Sacred!" reminded her of the divine union of Ardhanarishvara. Evelyn knew the story and told Pascal the story of the Indian god Annapurna," The Lord Shiva was the primordial destroyer of evil, the slayer of demons. He keenly observed the earth and was always rebuking and testing his wife's patience. Historically, the union between Shiva and Parvati was a glorious one. They maintained the equilibrium between thought and action on which the well-being of the world depended. Without his wife Parvati, the controller of the growth, transformation and energy in the world, Lord Shiva would only become a detached observer and the world would be extremely sparse. Their band formed a huge touch called Ardhanarishvara. Parvati was known as the Mother of the World for being equal, jubilant, and caring towards the world. Sooner or later, a rift would grow between these two formidable forces. Shiva hated the creations of goddess Parvati and Brahma and on earth, all the day-to-day life things and creations were known as maya. In Shiva's latest rebuke to his wife, Parvati knew that she had to prove to him the importance of her work. So, she took flight from this world, causing half of her cosmic to grow sparse with no food and on the other hand, Ardhanarishvara of Parvati began to collapse. Shiva knew that he was wrong, as everything on earth was sparse. Everyone was hungry and cold. Even he felt the absence of his wife and knew he could not be the only one who could sustain life. Parvati knew it was time for all the happenings to come back to normal and start a new life on earth. She went in the form of a new avatar called Annapurna, the goddess of food. She had a jewel-encrusted ladle and was carrying a golden pot filled with porridge. She was known as the goddess of food. She opened her own kitchen in the holy city of Kashi, on the banks of the

Gangas. She opened her kitchen to feed people and re-organize their health. Not only mere mortals came to the kitchen, but also Lord Shiva felt humble in his ways and thoughts and he went to Annapurna in the form of a poor beggar, begging for food and forgiveness. This way, Annapurna was the most rejoiced goddess of time and even now some of us remember her before eating".

Pascal was astonished by the explanation that came from the girl's mouth. He told her that he was mesmerized by the story and her vocabulary. But he didn't understand the connection between Annapurna and Monalisa.

Soon those two paintings of Monalisa arrived and Evelyn asked him," Have you done all the methods of finding the painter of Isleworth Monalisa?". "No", the technician confessed. So, Evelyn said," You can probably recreate the structure by John Asmus Pixel to get to know if his conclusion was right or wrong". Pascal happily nodded his head and asked her to help him. With her help, they went into many blogs of pixel art and he began recreating the Monalisa. As if by magic, the sizes of the pixels were correct, and the colour was exactly the same. So, John Asmus' conclusion was right. Suddenly, she had a perfect idea, which none of the scientists had ever thought of. She thought that the scientists were half-witted. She mumbled to herself," Why the scientists did not use the golden ratio method?". She did not break it out to Pascal but said, "In my ugly picture, there were dimensions in which two opposite hands were holding each other like Ardhanarishvara. Additionally, the shoulder joints between them look like a dimensional Rakshasha or a demon that Shiva killed. That's the connectivity between them".

She begged Pascal to let her look around the lab. Pascal nodded and said," This was quite an explanation, so as a reward, you get to look around". So Evelyn looked around his lab. It was very small and didn't have any machines except his invention and few computers and some portions. She happily skipped over to his invention, the first multispectral high definition camera. She bumped into Pascal after a round and snatched the Isleworth Monalisa.

She kept it on the stand and photographed it. Then, she took over his computer and searched Leonardo's red paint procedure for making it. She was a bit of a computer whiz. When it failed to understand, she despondently drummed her finger against the table and had an immediate good idea. Her favourite scientist was Martin Kemp as well and she cleverly used Google to make a video call.

Martin immediately came on a call and was pleasantly surprised at seeing the young girl. Evelyn conveyed to him the entire happenings and her feelings about Monalisa. He was impressed by the young girl's thought process of using the golden ratio method to significantly find out who had painted the Isleworth Monalisa. He was also impressed by her knowledge and charm. She asked him whether there were more than the Isleworth and they wanted to find out. Martin said that he wanted to try to paint a formidable character in his own painting and was trying to research more about Leonardo's painting. Evelyn was given the business to figure it out.

Soon, Martin Kemp said bye to Evelyn and terminated the call. Evelyn took a deep breath and began going over a rack of newspapers. She took a few interesting newspapers and sat down to rest. Meanwhile, Pascal was going through research to know who the Isleworth's sitter was. Somehow, Evelyn had the patience to browse the pages of the newspaper for the Monalisa facts, but sadly, she had become too attached to the comic section. She wanted to help Martin with his project of painting a person. When she read the comics, she saw another story related to the gods.

She read that there was once a Greek god named Hephaestus, the god of fire, who had breathed life into a baby girl. The baby girl was named as Pandora. God Zeus gave her two gifts. Pandora had a mind full of curiosity and at last she was gifted with the enormous green box. Zeus warned her not to open the box, as it was not for mortal eyes. Pandora was also an easily distracted girl, but she loved nature on earth. Later, she became more obsessed with trying to open the box and then, when curiosity got over her, she opened the box where the rattling sound called the name Pandora. Apparently, Zeus wanted to block the demons from entering the box, but when Pandora opened, every single demon came out, causing havoc on the earth. Again, when she shut the box, a soothing voice called out to her and she opened it again. A warm glow filled the box and a sickle came out of the box. Soon, in the next generation, a warrior named Perseus killed the deadly Medusa, but out of her neck came two children. One of them was Chrysaor, who was a giant who posed as a warrior. The second child was a beautiful horse, Pegasus. The pegasus could purify anyone. One day, a Greek prince went to the temple of Anthena, the goddess of war and wisdom, who gave him a golden bridal that helped him get the Pegasus to his aid. The prince practiced a war battle day and night, hoping that the gods on Mount Olympus could welcome him. One day, his battle training went wrong and he accidentally killed his brother. He was sent to the king of Argos to purify him, but something went terribly wrong. He soon killed his brother accidentally and he was sent to fight with a beast but was later killed after defeating the beast. Later, the abduction of the goddess of the earth's daughter, which later caused seasons for the planet, allowed her to spill tears for the death of the Greek prince.

Evelyn liked the story so much that she thought she could spill her emotions for it. Happiness, laughter, sadness, etc. rushed to her. If her emotions were mainly like that, even Monalisa made people cry because her tragic ending was mimicking people's laughs, and looking at her made everyone joyful. Suddenly, she got an amazing idea, this way, she could know if Monalisa was actually connected with all her stories.

Sadly, the Greeks did not work, as any common letters of all the Greek god's names doesn't match with the word Monalisa, but only the Indian stories had a connection with Monalisa. The reasons are:

1. Indians sometimes wore a veil around themselves in pregnancy that is exactly what Lisa del Giocondd wore, who was the sitter for the Monalisa. Lisa was expecting her second child, and her gift was the portrait(Monalisa).
2. Due to Monalisa's awkward pose, the Indian mythology story of Ardhanarishvara was matching.
3. She looked tan like an Indian. Analytically, the common letters I and A in Ardhanarishvara, Shiva, and Parvati matches with Monalisa's I and A.

Evelyn felt sad after all; she thought she had done so much research for it. She was about to have another go when she took a deep breath and said to herself," The Monalisa may have many problems, but there must be a solution, which I will do after dinner".

Later, she wrote a few numbers, which were seven and two(the numbers decoded inside the Monalisa). She handed over the paper to Pascal and went to the edge of the room, placed her hand on her chest, and said,"Leo! Take me home". Leo opened his jaws, and she was transported back home. It was the perfect time for dinner, and after the cold breeze of Paris, she was very much looking forward to sitting near the warm fire. But morosely for her, she was sent outside to check on her sister. Who knows, maybe one day or another Evelyn will be back for the case!

GREEK	INDIAN
Peg*a*sus	Parv*a*th*i*
Heph*a*estus	Sh*iva*
Pandor*a*	
Zeus	
Perseus	
Chrys*a*or	

MONALIS*A*	MONAL*ISA*
NO COMMON LETTERS OF ALL THE GREEK GODS MATCHES WITH MONALISA	LETETRS A and I Of Indian god(Shiva and Parvathi) matches with Monalisa.

Meanings:

Golden ratio: it is a mathematical relationship and ratio discovered and commonly found in nature, but which is visible almost everywhere, like in music, paintings, and so on. When used effectively, it creates designs that are naturally and aesthetically appealing to the eye by way of their artistic composition.

H.Yashnashree

POEMS

H.Yashnashree

Poem 1:
The perfect summer break

The wind is low

The flowers are bloomy

And no one is gloomy

And everyone is happy

The sun is hot.

The sea is cool.

And there is no school.

That's a very perfect summer break.

The sun is shining brightly.

Everything is going rightly.

Everybody loves the day.

To enjoy going to the sea or bay.

All the children says to the sun," Dear sun, always come and shine on us so we can play".

The sun replies," Yes dear children. I will always shine and that is the only way ".

The children tie their swings

To look up at the sky to see the birds flying using their wings

The king (Mango) season is here

It is a fruit but not a mortal mere

The tender coconuts are sweet

The birds sing and tweet

And no one gets freezed

The butterflies eat honey coated nectar

The bees make delicious honey

Everyone makes money

And goes to a vacation

We go to the beach

And eat mangoes and peach

The sand is rough

The sea is cool and wet

We all sunbathe on the sand

And sometimes it is like a friendship band

While sunbathing we put on our floppy sunhats

And our sunscreen is like a sunglasses

We all eat ice creams,popsicles and mocktails Icecream makes us scream Yippee!

The summer camp has started

H.Yashnashree

And the mangoes are being carted

Now what a happy summer break is this WOHO!

The Treasure Trove of Stories and Poems

Poem 2:
I go to the city of Paris

I go to the city of Paris

I like cafes but not buffets

Hey, It is time for a beach

Let there be no leach

I go to the city of Paris

Paris is the city of love

It flies like a dove

Sipping a cappuccino coffee

I want to savour a toffee

I go to the city of Paris, in France

Where I can dance

I go to the city of Paris

I go to the café and eat macron

When, in the sky, shines the moon

I see the Eiffel Tower

Wonder about its power

I go to the city of Paris

Picking fashion as a model I love Paris.

The Treasure Trove of Stories and Poems

H.Yashnashree

Poem 3:
AN AMUSEMENT DAY

I know! I know! I know I know! I know! I know

My cousins are playing outside

The road is wet, and the concrete is wide.

The sun is not bright

Inspite, inspite, inspite

I am reading a book

In a corner nook.

Sipping a cup of coffee

Seeing my sister sucking toffee.

Its enough!

I look out of the book roughly

Hmm! What a book! I was visualising the book scene.

That made me very keen.

I got up and wore my raincoat

There was a moat Suddenly, a big wave hit me

And someone pushed me into the moat, Whee!

But happily, my raincoat is sturdy for water.

My brother(the prankster) was a coward, but now he has catered.

I furiously wiped my sleeve on his hair

But still, we were one naughty and happy pair.

I ran home and revealed my new plot for one new gumboot

But I have got a sunny yellow puss in boots

I splashed in puddles

I didn't care, even when I was muddled.

My gumboots had thick soles

And they are very strong as poles.

The birds happily put their beaks into the lotus moat.

As little children, we made paper boats

Soon bloomed a tiny lotus

As children went to school safe and warm, seeing the lotus on the bus.

There was a sea of umbrellas, like a crowd

H.Yashnashree

Some are oval, some are round

What s lot of flashing colours!

Dancing in the rain with umbrellas is also a culture.

It was such a good day, we should not be bad

We should make sure the tear river does not come because of playing with matchsticks or iPads.

Out of a brick house comes a cute pup

Yup! And finally, the rain stops

A boy comes out with a leash

The dog's fur is peach

How curly it is!

See! It catches the ball in a whiz

I wish I could play with them too

Don't you wish to?

The Treasure Trove of Stories and Poems

H.Yashnashree

Poem 4:
My chicks

I have two roosters

Who are my energy boosters

They flap their wings

And hear music ding

I have two I won't give it to you (robbers)

One is the yellow a funny fellow

One is the pink who is clever to think

They love to play

And have fun with clay

We also play catch I go to my badminton batch.

They love shoes that are rubber

They have a big fat of blubber

You are my precious gem, not only you but also we

You should learn but also see.

You are the sun, the moon, the stars that shine brightly.

The Treasure Trove of Stories and Poems

You are nature, trees, flowers, and plants that grow rightly.

You should learn manners and discipline, and have the self-confidence to win.

Not to go to a resort or an inn.

Your faith lies in your hand.

It doesn't appear using a magic wand.

You should learn how to be polite.

And fill the happiness with light.

H.Yashnashree

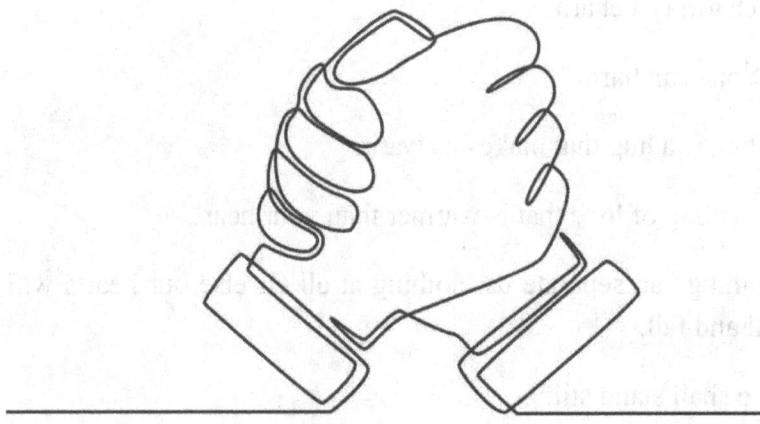

Poem 5:
Friendship day

A band that ties around

Tightening the edges safe and sound.

The band grows harder to break

We are free to the friends we seek.

A charm is a charm

No one can harm.

A hug is a hug that makes us warm

A feeling of love that is warmer than your heart.

Nothing can separate us, nothing at all Or else our hearts will fall and fall.

We shall stand still

Our hearts know why we will.

It does not mean we should be the same

Even the same language, nearby houses which are lame.

Everything is unique in our own way

A friend is there to show us the right way.

When we are gloomy

H.Yashnashree

They make it bloomy.

Are moods the same?

Which will never go into a blame.

You have my trust

A sword within my heart encrust.

We always share

Even the danger we are aware.

Happy Friendship Day

Poem 6:
Independence Day and freedom

Independence Day is in August.

A heart we could trust

We were invisible and rusty.

And rocks that had crumbled crust.

We wished a day would come.

Our sacrifices were gruesome.

We felt our whole world came to an end.

And we could not defend.

August 15th was the day.

Saving us from dismay.

How could we make ourselves proud?

Everyone thought we were as delicate as clouds.

The Emperor of India was treating us as slaves.

Watching us work for him while we had brainwaves.

George VI, monarch, and Victoria I, with customary titles

The Treasure Trove of Stories and Poems

Not one, but a bundle.

He loved to brag.

Hunt and eat, helping the poor.

Civil disobedience against the law

Not a flaw.

We protest, mutiny politics

There is no need if you have intelligent physics.

The British Raj was the rule.

To get the British crown on a schedule.

It lasted from 1858 to 1947—a lifetime.

It was the place of prime

India was covered with sadness.

We were not spacious.

The palace was to the east.

Where the king would have his feast

Running along his sword

Talking by his word.

H.Yashnashree

Father of the nation

You make a decision.

You are always right.

So we believe and fight.

Mohandas Karamchand Gandhi, we salute

On October 2, 1869, you were born as you.

Netaji, the hero

Who did not go back to the shadow?

The young wing of Congress died.

He did not say a single lie.

Subash Chandra Bose is so brave.

He came to the world to save.

Annie to the rescue

Running the New India newspaper with you.

Congress's first female president

Correct 100 percent.

British Annie Besant was to fight

India was closed tight.

The poet is renowned.

Her talents were hidden, not found.

Soon, she was fighting for us.

And did not care if we made a fuss.

Indian National Congress in 1925 (five)

Independence was chosen, as she had tried.

Why August 15?

Where pleading to get out of the country didn't work

And India's real shadow was about to lurk.

"I am tired" was not cribbing.

As the words in my mind were zipping

Lord Mountbatten was thinking that he had to get rid of this war.

And had passed the bill to the words he swore.

There is no power to transfer if there is no bloodshed.

So, August 15th, 1947, is what we have pled.

H.Yashnashree

The flag was flying on top of the red fort.

Now, the flag is flying because of our support.

This is our 76th year of independence.

First, it was zero, but we have this independence with our freedom fighters' help.

Jai Hind!

Jai Bharat Mata Ki Jai

H.Yashnashree

Poem 7:
Teacher's Day

All teachers are gods to us as we must be thankful for giving us the life savings that we need day to day, KNOWLEDGE.

You treat us with wisdom

Our school is the kingdom

You teach us subjects to learn

When are grades get higher you teach us a new turn

For knowledge we shall fight

And keep doing it again till we get what was right

Day or night

Knowledge in sight

You teach us math

And show us the path

You teach us English

Like a shooting star to make a wish

You teach us science

And manage our obedience

You teach us kannada

The language sounds like cultural mandala

You teach us hindi

Cold ,autumn or windy

You don't mind the weather.

And you are as light as a feather.

You teach us skits.

Which goes from knowledge to wits.

You teach plays

If we don't get it, you show us the way.

"Happy teacher's day"

H.Yashnashree

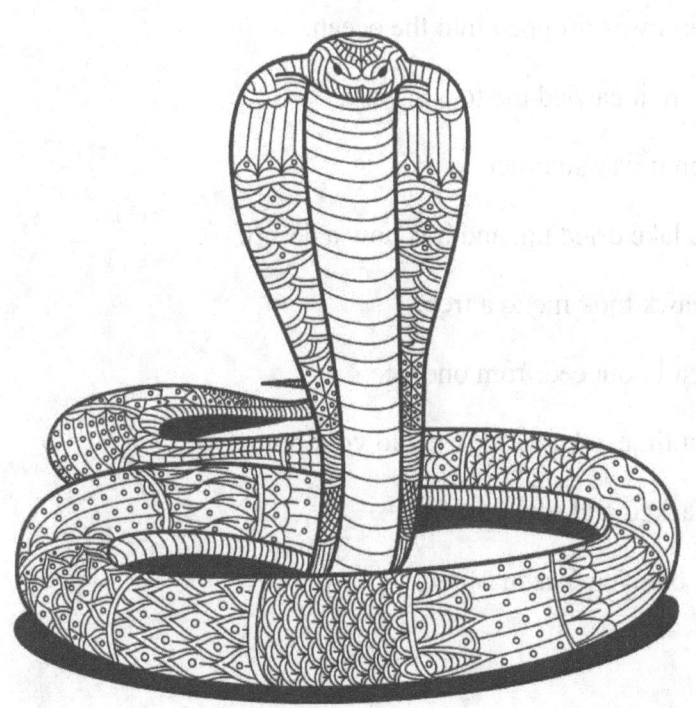

Poem 8:
The Talking Blue Taipan

I was in the northern mountains.

When a hawk came and scooped me the egg.

Then I was dropped into the ocean.

Where it carried me to a big sea.

Then it was summer.

The lake dried up, and it is now a desert.

A hawk took me to a tree.

Then I bounced from one tree.

That time, a hawk took me to your house.

I cracked and saw you.

My beloved Yashnashree!

H.Yashnashree

Poem 9:
The natural garden and wonders of emphatize

The fear of dust that soars through the mist

Cyclones of panic take a twist.

Trying to get happiness to the coast

As sadness vanishes away the most

Every time to get it through

And respect for peace is breaking through.

All the negatives of us go to positive

And everything has a motive.

As we can show in the future

The overcome of shyness is shattered through humour.

Making a one-and-only motto

You can tell that by your positive photo.

Representing every act of kindness like a water drop

Just like only one can save a crop

Searching for the beauty of the woodland

H.Yashnashree

The empathy dreams have been a schism of sand.

Only if we were generous enough to complete the day

Happiness and gratitude have to go their way.

The Adam's apple of knowledge is nothing but the wisdom in your brain.

As the peacock loves to dance in the season of rain

The summer season is always jolly.

When it is almost over, we say, "Oh golly."

When it is usually rainy season

The days are fat and petulant.

You even feel grouchy as an infant.

During the winter season, that is gelid.

The sadness in the heart has melted.

Every season has different features.

Even a single creature

But do not change.

Your unique range

Every person must act as a bridge.

For happiness, we must be the ridge.

Poem 10:
Grandparents day

I admire you the most.

Though you knew a lot, you never boasted.

You are always on my side.

And your heart is open and wide.

You are my lord.

You love to phrase in words.

You always try stuff.

And you neither give up nor make a fuss.

Your class is so good.

And you maintain every class under your hood.

You write lovely-hearted poems that come from your mind.

That raises your words and the sunshine through it, which makes us blind.

This makes me happy to think about how wonderful it is to have a grandma like you.

I love you grandma.

You are always careful with me.

But that is different from what everyone sees.

It shows that you love me.

And you always play with me when you are free.

You are the best.

You always tell stories while we rest.

We play business, Uno Kitchen set, don't you know?

You are sappy.

I am happy!

I love you grandpa

A life without you does not have any memories to litter

You sparkle at any time like glitter.

You always spread the love, young or old

As you tell us the amazing tales which were not told.

As you are my sun and moon

Any time as you are even my melodious tune.

You, grandparents, see us with a different pair of eyes

Your gentle talk is as the rain in July.

Your pleasure poem for the day

Happy GRANDPARENTS DAY

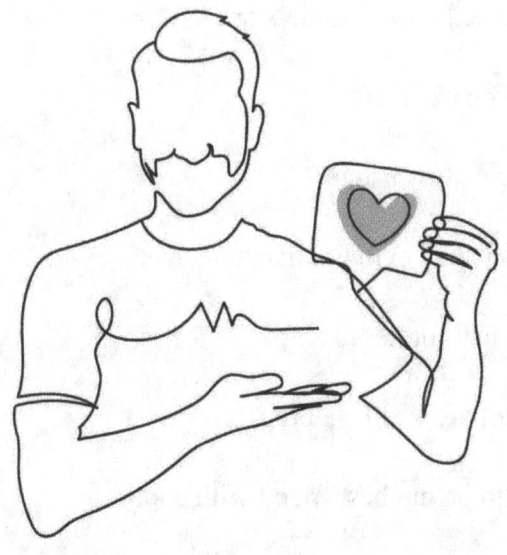

Poem 11: Inside shows

I used to know a girl who found me innocent.

That pride was higher, making her magnificent.

She tried to steal others' hearts.

By trying to act very smart

She possessed other people's art.

Which made her thefts start.

I wish she had no badge.

Because she had evilness like a madge.

I only wished for her to stop.

But she utilizes us like a prop.

She used to be my best friend with another

We used to be together, even in the summer.

She is pure and mean.

And she acts like a drama queen.

Betraying every single one of us

We were getting along with the fuss.

H.Yashnashree

With her curly locks

She loves to irritate and mock.

Through her rudeness, we can't tell apart

We must teach people like her to have a golden heart.

I would strictly like to be forbidden from people like her.

It is my advice, as per.

The Treasure Trove of Stories and Poems

Poem 12: Shyness

I am squawking with fear

I wish the ground would swallow me whole

As I am awkwardly stiff with the person near,

I feel myself shrinking with my goal.

I feel like touching my wish cloud

About being alone

That the wish would sprout

Being appalled inside my eggshell of stone

My thoughts drifted to the unknown

A place where it could rub my mind out of it

Were the voice in my head changed its tone

The place that kept my mind off it was the lonely voice in my wit.

Now I feel like a crumbled paper

Feeling the freeze of my bone

And the loneliness of vapor

I still do not find my true friends as mediocre as cyclones.

When my true destiny came to be with a friend who never abandoned me,

We were inseparable

As you could see, her voice was as sugary as ghee

And those memories were memorable.

H.Yashnashree

Poem 13:
A dirty fellow yellow shows his turn to shine

My rival says she likes purple.

I think it is illegal.

She says it means royalty.

I think I don't like that inside reality.

I reminded my favorite color means imaginative It is passionate.

The meaning of unity Joining friends and the community

The main element is right above our heads, feeling something, yellow lovers feel.

You will have to believe me, please; it is a deal.

So you feel it in your body before the air

Which parts to all, where we share

Our wealth in colors and trust

That color never rusts.

Others are also dashing, but we are not here to judge.

If we say, other colours won't budge

Feeling the warmth strangling around our body

H.Yashnashree

The sun is used to grow crops when the grass is knotty

We deceive the bright colors around us, which soak us down.

Our yellow carrier is focusing on the town.

Which shades with shadows like a long gown

Sometimes, which forms a frown

To all the yellow lovers around the world

Please spread the word.

Yellow is also a courageous color waiting to show up.

The Treasure Trove of Stories and Poems

Poem 14:
Widow's sorrow

The sun shades the dormitory through the school windows.

Down floating a lonely feather made of a widow

Through the clouds, trying to sketch it out

The widow bird is watching the feather, and then she pouts.

Dapling the dew, ejecting the rainbow bubbles

Then the trouble doubles.

Was she going to let the remains of hers sog down?

As she watched the pearly white sales of the river coated with brown rock,

Despite her agony, let her remain.

Let her sorrow go for now.

Beyond that, she feels happy.

And sappy

Poem 15:
Something no one knows…

The love you gave to us

Is heart melting and thus

When you two were born

In a normal farm

You can change any heart into gold.

It is the legendary story never told.

They can look into other's hearts to find kindness or not.

It is a very great deed that does not rot.

All of us have personal issues that they can understand.

They comfort our feelings, removing the fear we cannot withstand.

As a routine of play

They play in the mud all day.

There are many varieties of dishes they like.

They get a wacky idea every time their face lights up and strikes.

They can't resist the taste of cheese and mealworms.

Sometimes, they steal it but also get it when something salient is to earn.

They love to tempt themselves with grains.

For that, they have the longest history of a food chain.

They have their own directs in gardening here are the steps.

Step 1: Accidentally push off their grains from the box.

Step 2: Roll the grains that fell out into the soil. (PS: Make sure boulders are further from the plants than the rocks.)

Step 3: Poop on the grains, as they are natural fertilizers used for the soil.

Step 4: Heavy rain can make them grow faster, and herbivores should not toil.

Step 5: Keep the plants healthy. To make them wealthy (love) To my dearest and most loving roosters, Sunshine and Meadow.

Poem 16: Determination but feisty

All the colors swirling in my heart

I don't know what's beaten me to the part.

But no matter how much I play, I always miss a shot.

I will never throw the passion in my heart to rot.

I always get it once or twice.

I try my best to work, rolling like a dice

Trying to get it right

Through it, I fight.

My eyes are full of determination.

Trying to succeed on this occasion I remember that we should try until we succeed.

But not filled with greed.

The Treasure Trove of Stories and Poems

H.Yashnashree

Poem 17:
Adventure in reading

Colors splashing everywhere make up the wild.

The forest floor is so green, blooming with blossoms.

The temperature is coloring it to make it mild.

Soon, bursting with life is awesome.

With the click of my heel

High I jump

Crossing the pages of the book reveals

Skipping over the pages as stumps

I come to a different place in a book.

Washing with overhead city lights

From every corner to every nook

Being a carnival of beautiful sights

This is the feeling of being inside a book.

Reading is the adventure from every nook and cranny.

Poem 18:
Inner qualities pulverized or not

Do you feel the pain?

Jumbling through our confidence.

Just when something goes wrong.

The idea thrives but fades away.

Feeling there was no chance of getting towards it.

Unable to track it down, paving through our hearts that we would never do it again.

Footsteps leading us to paradise enter our hearts, as the other, blinding us with a second chance of promising success.

Skipping all the way towards it on the promising soul, but before we enter, there is a prong of destiny to be received.

Refreshing ourselves into another chance is the ticket of wisdom.

The colors of the rainbow affect us as it lead us to the final pot of gold.

Which holds the success in hand and the flames of the final ends.

There is a piece of heart an extreme voyager could seek.

H.Yashnashree

The most powerful thing to hold in the brain is known as wisdom. Though you rush across the mountain or swim along the sea.

Or mine the way through and get something precious, which does not make sense.

If you have the wisdom and the humanity to pass.

It is a shame that no one can be near you unless you are ready to befriend them.

The Treasure Trove of Stories and Poems

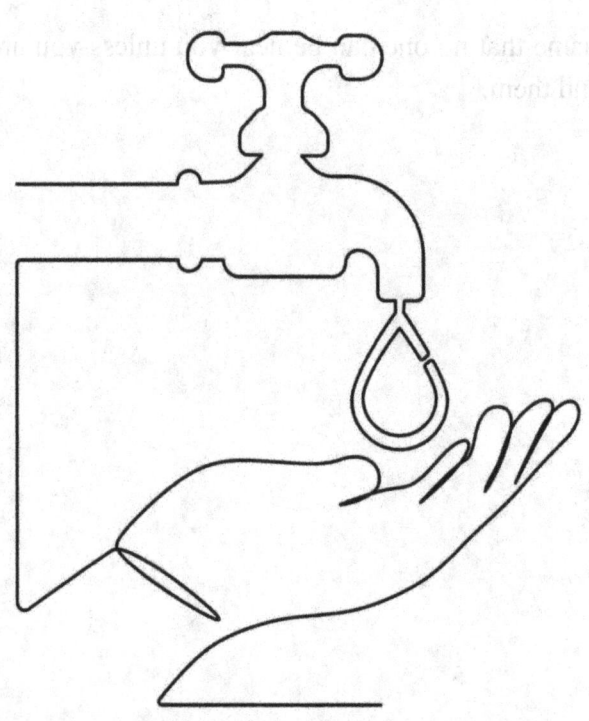

H.Yashnashree

Poem 19:
A drop can save a life

A single drop of water

Can save a life

Reflecting rainbows through it

Shading us from the boiling-hot

Approaching the waves to the surface

Giving us a present as we sit along the waves

It is seashells!

As the moon looks upon the water facing itself

Wondering that below the sea is a unique quality

Not understanding leaves it alone, as the sun might crack it.

But neither did the sun know.

When it was evening, the sun and moon sat together.

They decided it meant that water gives life.

Everyone always includes water in all their meals.

So if there is less water, there is less life.

H.Yashnashree

Poem 20:
The pearly exchange

On October 28, the second eclipse was a rare occasion after 14 days of solar eclipses.

October is a month of celestial events such as solar eclipses, meteor showers, and finally the lunar eclipse.

The positioning of the earth between the sun and the moon is when the lunar eclipse occurs.

It also comes due to the full moon while we slumber.

As the three celestial bodies' exact alignment is not guaranteed

It does not stay in a straight line to win our hearts and succeed.

The surface of the moon is given away by the earth's shadow is umbra

The moon's other parts are covered by the outer part of the earth's shadows, is penumbra.

In 2023, October 29th, at 1.05 am, is when the time begins.

At 2.24 am, the time ends, and some birds start their song of the violin.

Gradually, the eclipses begin and will turn a reddish or copper color nicknamed as blood Moon.

It is like a breath-taking cartoon.

We must simply avoid physical activities.

Or that can lead to heart problems or accidents, according to the myth, because of the activities.

In some cultures, people try to restrain

From eating to drinking during the eclipse, it makes us insane.

The bad darkness of the sky falls upon us.

As a myth, pregnant women must stay inside or something bad might happen to the unborn child, and thus,

We must not fall asleep during the eclipse.

As we get 30% of deep sleep as the lights break at dawn, during an eclipse

Eclipses are also known as a bad omen.

It is when the demon god Rahu, who is as deadly as a bowman,

Grapples the sun and moon in his mouth.

Being a demon god, it gives out a negative light from the north to the south.

We must take an immediate bath after the lunar eclipse.

To help reduce the dreadful effects of the lunar eclipse

H.Yashnashree

The mark of your wound if you fall on a lunar eclipse might stay forever.

Any time, whenever

I really wish the myths were not real, as they scare many people out of their wits.

It must not be permitted.

H.Yashnashree

Poem 21:
Diwali Celebration

Little tufts of light float in the air.
It shines and, thus, is very fair.
The pots are brown and baked.
By the holy oil, which is sacred.
Virtue and reality destroy lunar systems as they dare.
Slowly but firmly, the sun comes because of the lamps, I swear.
The celebration is also because Rama kills Ravana, brings victory, and brings his wife Sita back.
Then as of Rama's victory, they crowned him king in enthusiasm in lakhs.
If I were him, I would concentrate as I hold the bow.
Hoping for mankind, hitting Ravana with a shot, then falls down to the gods with a bow.
The rows of lights sometimes bear garlands.
Because it is when Lord Vishnu and Lordess Lakshmi celebrate their wedding on a plot of land.
Or it could be Goddess Lakshmi's birthday arrival or Krishna killing Narakasura.
Killing is the blood of a demon, which is a god's aura.
This is how the aura of celebration and happiness is cherished by us.
Everyone will meet, greet, and fuss.
We can stop everyone from being noise-polluted by loud music and sound.
By spreading awareness, to each and everyone found
We must get rid of firecrackers.
And spread awareness so the news will be in the world, not only for the people who have listened to me to gather.
I hope you have a noisy free Diwali.
And a merry Diwali

H.Yashnashree

Poem 22:
The Whispers Of Tears

Do you feel the pain as I do?
Through your face, I see the pain.
You just wondered why you walked away.
Leaving me alone through the soberly place.
Could you just turn back and realize the mistake we made.
Our hearts just break into two pieces.
I feel like coming after you and throwing myself at you.
I really wish I could count the time backward.
I hate to feel the way we are really stuck.
With no one else to reassure as a pat on the back.
I just felt dumped as I am.
Wishing my tears was my reflection of bringing us close.
You too, just felt so hard to stay.
Feeling restless while sitting in one place
We both just wanted to come back together and solve things.
We didn't know that more tears would come as it wiped away the courage of love.
And embarking ourselves to come together.
Feeling shaken in fury with a little glow in our eyes
Trying to guide us to our hearts
And find ourselves happy, and....................we hug!
I was inspired when my sister and I fought with each other.

H.Yashnashree

Poem 23: Time is valuable

Every single day is a respect for the next one.
There are many days you never want to pass.
But there are days when you wish it would go.
You can't help that pitiful behaviour on time.
But there are some days when good and bad happen.
Some days we get influenced by dreadful people.
Some days we get under good influence.
Time is passing very fast.
We must start changing everything from bad to good memories.
Time is running fast.
Do we have time to change?

Poem 24:
Happy Thanks Giving

Thanks to all the janitors at school.

Thank you for everything.

You have a place in our hearts

We can have a determined face and overcome

Any obstacles through your hard work.

You are the one who also has the best heart.

We feel the pain as you do

You know what is best for our school

You care for each of our antics

Without you, we would not be in such a great position.

I notice the hard work you put in when you braid for girls

In your limited free breaks, you make up for any mess

In the realm of soothing words, you come across some of our morose faces

And you are the one, we can say as a great example

That all jobs are respected equally.

The Treasure Trove of Stories and Poems

H.Yashnashree

Poem 25:
The wounds of courage

I have many, many wounds.

They all leave a scar.

It suffers from lots of bounds.

As the blood comes out, so far

It hurts, but I always smile.

But sometimes, it leaves a bitter mark.

As it pains, it piles.

But I am proud to show it.

I never cry when I get a wound as big as a shark.

I feel the startled faces of people.

But as I am proud to fall, from that, I will rise again.

Poem 26: Obstacles

Through the twinkling of the stars is a set of obstacles.

The valley of obstacles cannot be entrenched, so it can be accomplished by using the amruta of knowledge and the determination of a person.

Being determined and not panicking is the first step to crossing an obstacle.

Each one of us has a goal that cannot be fulfilled by greed and misery.

It can be achieved through passion.

Though it is the toughest goal in the world

We don't seem to fear the lack of discouragement and unhappiness around us.

It doesn't seem to be the same.

When we fear a lot, it is time to Change and start facing a new obstacle.

The Treasure Trove of Stories and Poems

H.Yashnashree

Poem 27 :
Chase to be cherished

Casting wishes on petals so small.
Chasing dreams so tall.
Imagination flies high, like a bird in the sky.
The child's mind has more than meets the eye.

As the petals of great desire sway.
I also know that they should never get old and frayed.

We are only tender saplings and our mind is fresh.
It's time for some knowledge of imagination to refresh.

There is something that can enclose the gloom.
It is the variety of flowers that bloom.

Red, yellow, orange, white—you name it.
We have the reasons behind it to benefit.

Red for goals and orange for passion.
Yellow for dreams and white for imagination.

Teachers like you can sprout these in us.
It might take a long time and thus.

We would let our minds wander to the furthest location in the universe.
Could we go to a limited extent where it would be bare with a portal?

Our minds are engrossed in the beauty of the portal and we all wonder what would be in there, big or small?

Some of us stay devoted to nurturing vines.
While we cogitated on what the reason was behind the wonderful floral land and sunshine.

Wishes, dreams, goals and imagination are spread out in a meadow.
There we find our glory, all because we are being sown.

We are provided with a place to reorganize ourselves.
We have faith and we pass down our qualities by being wise.

There flowed a river.
That snaked and shivered.

The calm lake was a mirror.
Of the beauty of a picture.

But more than water, there was a lake.
Fitted with words that described the passion of a child that never breaks.

It would go rhythmically and was very sweet.
Who would describe the nectar of the imagination but a child who is complete.

Complete is nothing but full of goals that attempt to reach the sky.
Not with colourful wings that fly.

However, the mind has different variations of thought processes.
It doesn't cause stress.

Chasing goals is not about touching a shimmering orb or making your hands absorb.
But make your goals achievable.

Poem 28:
Who am I?

Lead is soft and grey.
It makes your stick never fray.
It comes with smooth curves.
Which it deserves
Who am I?
……..
I am a pencil.
Sometimes in pastel with colours.
But never duller.
Yellow, purple, blue, etc.
Every colour has a hue.
Who am I?
…….
I am a crayon.
Soft, rubbery, and squeezy
Some are feeling cheesy.
Making disappear
And not appear
Who am I?
…..
I am an eraser.
I can see the number.
I can remember
To go to nine
It is fine.
Who am I?
……

I am a scale.
It can show the thickness on boards.
Use to show sums and records
Who am I?
…
I am a marker.
I make the lead sharp.
From top to scrap
I can give it double size.
But I better be wise.
(Because the pencil becomes small)
Who am I?
….
I am a sharpener.
But water mostly and I come to life.
You don't have to scrape me with a knife.
As I give colour
I can also change into many shades.
Who am I?
…
I am paint
I clean up the mistakes using liquid.
But in schools, I am restricted.
People use me at home.
And I am the size of a gnome.
Who am I?
…..
I am whitener.
On a stick, liquid comes out.
From the nib, which pouts
In that, there is a hole.
With an on or off pole.

H.Yashnashree

Who am I?
…..

I am a pen or ink pen.
A box to place things
With your heart leaping with wings
Who am I?

……..

I am a geometry box.
I record every thought and wish.
That is ready to jump out like a fish.
But I am bound shut.
To stay put
Who am I?

……

I am a diary.
I mark every word as useful.
And I am very truthful.
Who am I?

…..

I am a highlighter.
I am used to cutting things.
My handles are shaped like wings.
Once I cut through the material
Your art will become real.
Who am I?
I am a scissors.
You can apply me to anything and we will stick together.
My stickiness is as light as a feather.
You can use me for the artwork, etc.
And everyone in this world uses me—my luck.
Who am I?

….

The Treasure Trove of Stories and Poems

I am glue.
I have many symbols of numbers, and I am used for accounts.
Don't think I cannot count.
Because I am smarter than an average human brain span
If you do not believe me, you can use me to scan [numbers].
Who am I?
…..
I am a calculator.

Printed in the USA
CPSIA information can be obtained
at www.ICGtesting.com
LVHW031921140924
790863LV00016B/1133